"Bella, we have a matter of business to discuss."

She was instantly alerted by the deliberate coolness with which he spoke.

Recklessly, she said, "You need not be so mysterious about this matter of business, Tony. As it happens, I believe I know what you wish to discuss. It is marriage, is it not? I assure you, I am ready to discuss it this very instant."

"I cannot recall you ever evincing much interest in the subject before," he remarked.

She coloured. "Such a rich subject, matrimony. I believe there cannot be too much said about it."

He did not take up her gay tone. His look was severe. "It is not precisely marriage I wish to discuss, Bella."

"Not marriage? What then, my dear husband?"

"In point of fact, my dear wife," he said, "it is divorce."

Books by Barbara Neil

HARLEQUIN REGENCY ROMANCE
21–LESSONS FOR A LADY
30–THE CELEBRATED MISS NEVILLE
41–LUCY'S SCOUNDREL

BELLA

BARBARA NEIL

Harlequin Books

TORONTO • NEW YORK • LONDON
AMSTERDAM • PARIS • SYDNEY • HAMBURG
STOCKHOLM • ATHENS • TOKYO • MILAN
MADRID • WARSAW • BUDAPEST • AUCKLAND

To Marmie

Published April 1992

ISBN 0-373-31172-9

BELLA

PART ONE

Return of the Native

CHAPTER ONE

EVEN THOUGH her remarkable ivory back was to the door, Isabella knew the precise moment he arrived. It was not the eyes of her guests which warned her, for they were fixed on her with their customary admiration. Nor was it the footman's nasal announcement of the name Mr. Anthony Ashton, for she was too engrossed in conversation to hear it. What signalled his presence was the sudden blaze of heat which flushed her bare back. It caused her to shiver, as though a cold finger had touched her. She scolded herself for blushing like a green girl.

Because she had rehearsed this moment carefully, she took a breath to compose herself, affixed a brilliant smile to her lips and turned to face him. There was fatefulness in that turn, for she knew what he would see. All the snowy satin of her gown, all the burnished lustre of her upswept curls, all the sparkle of diamonds on her breast could not protect her. Two years had passed since Anthony Ashton had left England, and the ensuing time, care and sorrow had worked changes which would not escape him. He would see in an instant that she was no longer in the first blush of youth. She was a woman now: mature in her figure and confident in her carriage, though her heart had not changed.

He, she saw with a pang, had greatly improved during the time of their separation. His adventures in

the wilds of Canada had tanned and strengthened him.
Dressed in the plainest and finest style, he wore a coat
of smoky green, a simple white cravat and a pale green
brocade waistcoat. His stride as he approached was
sure. The passage of time had served to add depth to
his handsome features and dignify his bearing. He was
what he had always been, only more so: dark, elegant, penetrating and, most of all, ironic.

Despite the intervening months, the sight of that
ironic smile still filled Isabella with a sensation no one
else had the power to inspire—a sensation that lodged
somewhere between longing and fear. She had never
been able to put a name to it; she knew only that his
smile was as magnetic as it was enigmatic. There was
a time when she had gone to great lengths to pierce its
implacable irony. Now, however, she was resolved to
put such recollections from her mind. What was there
to fear, after all? Had he not returned to England?
Had he not come to see her? She threw back her
shoulders and met his steady gaze.

"My dear Bella," he said, bowing. He raised her
hand, letting it fall before his lips actually brushed her
glove. She tried to read his emotion in the set of his
jaw. For a moment she suspected that he regarded
their meeting with distaste; yet his manner was nothing if not cordial.

She had watched her hand in its progress towards
and away from his lips. When he let it go, she was
obliged to speak. "Well, it has been an age, hasn't it?"
she said lightly.

"You have not changed," he said. Although he
spoke politely, there seemed to Isabella a world of implication in the words: had he come back in the hope
that she had changed?

"Nonsense," she laughed. "Of course I have changed. I've acquired all the worst infirmities of advancing decrepitude, not the least of which are crow's-feet and a penchant for speaking fondly of yesterday's dinner."

He remained determinedly gallant. "You speak as though you were in your dotage, which, clearly, you are not. Even if you were ever to suffer such infirmities, they would no doubt serve to lend you character."

She replied ruefully, "By which you mean to say that I am currently lacking in character."

As he met her look, his expression was sardonic. "In essentials you are the same. You still possess that style which is uniquely your own. I observe, for example, that you continue to defy fashion as perversely as ever. While every other woman in the room exhibits her bosom, you show the world your back."

She bowed her head in acknowledgement of the compliment, pleased that he had noticed her back. It was a magnificent back; all the gentlemen of taste and fashion were agreed on that. Not many months before, a party of dashing young admirers had vied to see who could best describe its ivory smoothness in a rhyme. More than one portrait painter had begged to be allowed to translate its grace to canvas. If Ashton had been impervious to her back, she could not have borne it.

"What have you done with your Canadian cousins?" she asked. "I looked forward to meeting them."

"At your kind invitation, I have brought them here tonight. Now, with your permission, I shall present them."

He snapped a bow and walked away. As he disappeared through the crimson-curtained entrance, she became aware that fifty pairs of eyes stared at her; her guests had been watching her all the while. They had suspended their conversations, flirtations and assignations expressly to witness this meeting between herself and Mr. Anthony Ashton.

Isabella could not pretend surprise at the public attention, for she had gone to some trouble to arrange it. She had made certain that her first view of him and his of her should take place in the safety of a crowd. But even if she had not arranged a public meeting, she would have accepted the unabashed curiosity of her guests as wholly in the nature of things, for long ago she had embarked upon a career of standing the Town on its ear, and now, she knew, she was expected to produce something out of the way for her guests' entertainment. Ordinarily, she would have been quick to gratify that expectation, but now, having come face-to-face with Ashton, she yearned for a private moment. She wished to contemplate Ashton's determined smile and think what she might do to soften it.

All at once, everybody looked towards the entrance. There stood a young lady whose fair beauty conjured up visions of a mediaeval Madonna. It was a beauty not one whit diminished by the terror diffusing her pale oval face. Isabella knew that such a combination—beauty and terror—was exactly calculated to inspire the gentlemen of the Town to worship the girl who possessed them. But the young lady framed by the arch was not in the least calculating. Isabella had only to look at her once to know that this child was what she herself had never been: innocent.

As Isabella met the young girl's eyes, she saw them cloud with dread. Then suddenly, as those large eyes shifted to the polished floor, Isabella was struck with an idea. *The child is afraid of me,* she thought. She might have laughed out loud at such a preposterous idea had she not caught sight of the formidable lady who followed the girl, a handsome, tawny-complected female almost as wide as she was tall. She was clad in beaded deerskin hemmed by a fringe which reached to her ankles. About her coarse-braided hair was wound a band of blood red. Across her face spread a menacing expression which dared the company to mount an attack.

The guests had lined themselves on either side of a path leading from the entrance to the pillar by which Isabella stood. They watched every step the young girl and her exotic companion took. After a moment, they turned their heads to observe Isabella. Then, turning again, as though they were spectators at a game of lawn tennis, they gawked once more at the approaching twosome. Isabella was tempted to remark on the crowd's ridiculous gaping, but she knew the time was not right. It was a first principle with her to misbehave only when she might produce a stunning effect.

As she watched them approach, her notice was caught by the young man who accompanied them. He arrested her attention with the expression of fiery hatred he levelled at her. *He thinks I am an ogress,* she thought, and though she smiled at the absurdity, it cost her a pang, for his ill opinion had to be attributed to something Ashton had said of her.

Last to walk the gauntlet was Ashton himself. He appeared wholly unaware of the stares of the crowd. His air of perfect tranquillity contrasted sharply with that of the others. When he reached her, they all stood for a moment in silence.

Isabella stepped forward and in her best *grande-dame* manner took the girl's hand, saying in a soft, light-hearted tone, "You are welcome, my dear, and let me assure you that you are not poor Joan of Arc going to the stake. I may roast my guests, but I never burn them."

The girl swallowed hard, making a furious effort to comprehend her meaning.

With the barest smile, Ashton presented his cousin, Miss Celeste DuChateau. The girl curtsied unsteadily, gazing at Isabella with large brown eyes.

Blithely, Ashton continued, "And may I present Miss DuChateau's *yatoro,* her companion, Wild Goose, member of the esteemed Iroquois tribe."

Isabella paused to admire the costume, complexion and ferocity of the Indian woman, who glowered at her. "So pleased, Miss Wild Goose," she said.

"She is not *Miss* Wild Goose, Bella," Ashton corrected. "She is simply Wild Goose."

"Well, I cannot introduce her to my grandfather as a waterfowl, can I? You know what the Old Duke is. She must have a title of some sort."

"Does your grandfather still flatter himself that every worthy creature on the planet bears a title?"

"Unless she has a ladyship prefixed to her name, Grandpapa will never condescend to notice her."

"Well, as you object to Wild Goose, perhaps you would prefer to call her by her Indian name, Ahonk."

"Ahonk! I adore it. Its inelegance is quite wonderful. Still, Grandfather will prefer it if she has a title. Therefore, I shall supply her with one. Grandpapa need never know the truth."

"You are very wicked, Bella."

"I expect that comes as no surprise to you," she said, looking directly into his eyes, wondering if this boldness would shake his composure.

His smile remained as steady as stone.

"It is settled: Wild Goose shall be a princess," Isabella declared. "It is my understanding that all Indian ladies are princesses, and if they are not, surely they ought to be."

"By all means, elevate the lady," he said. "She is courageous and loyal and deserves every honour you can confer."

Addressing Wild Goose, Isabella said, "Will you like to be a princess? It would be most convenient."

In a monotone, Wild Goose replied, "I am agreeable."

"I certainly hope so," Isabella murmured fervently.

She then turned to the young man, who was introduced to her as Guy DuChateau, brother of Celeste. He clicked his heels in a bow which eloquently conveyed the iciest resentment.

Laughing, Isabella said, "If you persist in scowling, sir, I shall be forced to make you fall in love with me. The challenge is almost irresistible."

At this sally, he stared. When she extended her hand to him, he was too confused to do anything but bend over and kiss it.

"That was very prettily done," she told him, giving his arm a tap with her black lace fan. "If you continue to mind my instructions on proper behaviour and do everything I tell you, we shall get on splendidly."

On this, she turned from his astonished face to the waiting assemblage, which stared at them all in anticipation. She took a breath to stop the pounding of her heart and spoke in the most animated voice she could muster.

"Hush, everybody," she addressed the company, even though it had long ago fallen silent. Her voice floated through the expectant crowd in the ballroom like a melody played on a flute. "Permit me to introduce to your acquaintance a gentleman who has come back to us from a lengthy sojourn in Canada, where the principal society he sought was that of the trapper, the Indian and the beaver, a gentleman who brings with him his delightful cousins, the Sister and Brother DuChateau and their charming companion, a princess of the Royal House of Goose. Ladies and gentlemen, I present Mr. Anthony Ashton, renowned for his courageous exploits in the colonies and, incidentally, my husband."

She waited for that last heavy word to be absorbed. Not one of the guests needed to be told who Anthony Ashton was, but Isabella was compelled to state the fact to their faces, not so much for their sake as her own. It was as if an out-and-out declaration that she was Mrs. Anthony Ashton would magically restore her to her place in the world.

The result of her introduction was more comical than magical, however. Jaws hung and eyes bulged with curiosity. If she had been able to steady her heart, she would have laughed. From the guests' faces, she turned to Ashton's and attempted to read his expression. Did his smile denote amusement, or contempt?

Walking to him, she dipped a low curtsy, bowed her head and said so that all might hear, "You are welcome to Ashton House, sir. We rejoice that you have come home at last to your country, your house, and, most of all, your wife." Then she lifted her eyes to his and, with a coquettish look which she hoped would mask her trepidation, awaited his reply.

CHAPTER TWO

ASHTON CAST HIS EYES over the ballroom, which was so still that one might hear the noise of traffic in the environs of Hertford Street. A candle sputtered in the chandelier, sending a hiss through the charged air. Gravely, he handed Isabella up so that he might study her face. Her posing as a dutiful, submissive wife entertained him hugely. Slowly, he broke into laughter, with a low, soft laugh. Before long, it infected the gaping onlookers, who began to laugh with him, uncertainly at first, then raucously.

This was Bella at her best, Ashton thought: daring, witty, self-mocking. In the past, however angry he had felt, she had always had the power to make him laugh. Her other attractions were still just as potent, he acknowledged. That fact had struck him the instant he'd set eyes on her glorious back. But two years' separation—one of them in the company of the gentle Celeste—had surely made him proof against Bella's charms.

The laughter relieved the tension in the room. Soon the guests took up again the business of amusing themselves, and there was no want of matter for conversation, to be sure. Ashton conjectured that his return would form the sole topic of gossip for the rest of the evening, if not the Season.

"Why have the musicians stopped playing?" Isabella cried. "I shall go and scold them. Everybody

must dance. We have much to celebrate, do we not?''
On that, she glided away in the direction of the violins, and as he watched her go, Ashton received an impression of clinging satin, winking diamonds and bronze hair which fell in curls towards her glorious expanse of back.

After following her a moment with his eyes, he turned to Celeste to find her looking distressed. "Are you well?'' he enquired. "Are you fatigued? Shall I take you away?''

"I was quite terrified,'' the young lady replied. "I believe I am a little recovered now, for she made you laugh. That was well done of her, I think.''

"When Bella sets out to make one laugh, it is well nigh impossible to resist her.''

"I thought I should hate her and that I should blurt out something quite dreadful.''

He smiled at her innocent face. "Why should you hate her?''

"Because she made you unhappy.''

"I never said she made me unhappy. I never uttered her name that I recollect.''

"Your silence told me everything. But pardon me, I do not mean to speak of painful matters.''

"If I have been made unhappy, then *I* should be the one to hate her, but there is no cause for you to do so. And I must confess, I do not hate her. One cannot hate Bella, no matter how much one would like to.''

The strains of a dance burst from the violins. Ashton escorted Wild Goose to a pillar, where she folded her arms across her broad bosom and fixed her eyes on her young charge. Then, offering his arm to Celeste, he led her down to the set. The music was measured enough to permit his partner to practise the steps she had so recently learned. At the same time, he was permitted to gather his thoughts.

Taken all in all, this first meeting with Bella had begun well. He attributed its success to time, which had cast a thick haze over their marriage, a grey haze that, like the mist surrounding the English countryside, softened harsh lines and rendered them indistinct. Time and distance could not be equalled, he believed, for giving one perspective, and perspective was essential, for Bella's allure was still a force to be reckoned with.

"What are you thinking?" Celeste asked, bringing him back to the present. "You have been far away."

"I am thinking how strange it is to be in my own house once more."

"Is it very much changed?"

For the first time, he looked about him. Up to now, he had not noticed the particulars of his surroundings. There was, however, something disturbingly familiar in all of it, a softness of cream colours which recalled mornings spent watching Bella's face as she slept among the pillows and a scent of lily of the valley which he associated with the curve of her neck.

"I cannot tell whether it is greatly changed or not," he answered calmly enough, "but it does affect a man to come home after so long an absence."

"And seeing *her* again—that too must have its effect." As she searched his face, concern was visible in her expression.

He smiled, thinking, not for the first time, that this young cousin of his was the loveliest, best-hearted creature in the world. "I suppose it must."

"It is a great pity, I think," she said with a sigh.

Raising an eyebrow, he replied, "You do not pity Bella, I hope. She would not like that at all. Nor would I."

"Oh, I pity both of you!" she cried. Then, mortified at her outburst, she pleaded, "Forgive me. I did not mean to offend."

"It is not in your power to offend." He spoke in the gentle tone he reserved for Celeste.

He took her hand to execute a turn and waited while she counted her steps. When talk resumed, she said, "It is well that you do not hate her."

"Yes," he agreed, "and even better that I do not love her."

ISABELLA DISMISSED the young Corinthian by her side so that she might engage Guy DuChateau in conversation. That young man, who leaned against the wall with his arms folded, was occupied in glaring at all the world. Despite his sullens, she liked him. His determined coldness struck her as interesting. Not the least of his attractions was the resemblance she fancied she saw to Anthony Ashton.

"You must not scowl so," she whispered to him. "If you are to get on in London, you must learn that in proportion as one wishes to scowl, one must smile."

He regarded her with scorn. "I cannot act in a manner which contradicts my feelings."

"Then you must learn. You will never make a satisfactory entrée into Society unless you become adept at hypocrisy. Perhaps I shall teach you. I am thought to be skilled in the art. You may begin by asking me to dance."

He looked shocked.

Isabella assured him, "I am quite at liberty and you need have no fear of my refusing you."

"Perhaps I do not wish to dance."

"I am sure you could not possibly be so impolite, or so foolish."

His lips thinned. "I have only just learned your English dances. I am not certain of my steps."

"Then we shall converse instead. Conversation is very much like dancing. Both depend upon pre-scribed forms which maintain the motion. If one can catch the rhythm, the exercise yields a tolerable plea-sure. Now, what shall we talk of? I have it. I shall ask you a question: why do you dislike me so bitterly?"

"I beg your pardon?"

"I am sure I never harmed you in my life, and if I did, I am very sorry for it."

"You may spare yourself the trouble of conversing with me, Mrs. Ashton. I know what you are."

"Indeed? Has Tony spoken of me?"

"He has never spoken of you; I need know nothing further."

Earlier she had assumed that Ashton had spoken ill of her. Now she was alarmed to find that he had not so much as mentioned her name. "What do you imagine you know of me?" she asked.

"I expect you are the sort of female who likes to break hearts, who thinks only of her toilette and her gowns and who sneers at a gentleman's coat and con-versation if they do not precisely conform to the es-tablished mode."

Isabella glanced at his decidedly unfashionable coat, then smiled into his well-formed face. "Do you see me sneering? It seems to me I have behaved in a vastly civil manner to you and your sister, though I never set eyes on you before."

Guy's brows contracted. "You have no choice but to be civil to your husband's relations. No doubt you will sneer behind your fan at the earliest opportunity."

"You are mistaken," she said. "I have no desire to sneer at you. If any one is to be sneered at on this or any other occasion, it shall be myself."

Guy took several moments to absorb this warning.

Seeing that he had not caught her tone of irony, she said kindly, "I am not such a villainess as you make me out to be."

"Must I now regard you as a heroine because you have spent two minutes in my company without yawning?"

"I generally recommend looking for heroines in sentimental novels, of which I am a prodigious reader, though it is not the fashion, I know, to confess it. I assure you, I am not in the habit of looking down my nose at young gentlemen, even when their manners are perfectly execrable."

He reddened.

"I do not object to your disliking me. I do not object to anybody's disliking me. Indeed, to be liked by some is a positive curse. But I do wish you would take the time to become better acquainted with me before forming your opinion. Then, at least, I might have the opportunity of giving you good reason to dislike me."

He laughed, then caught himself. The dance ended, and the couples made their way towards the chairs. Along with the crowd of dancers, Isabella and Guy adjourned to a table where a tray of champagne had been set. Each took a glass, and after a refreshing sip, she glanced at the face of her companion to find him studying her.

"You are the oddest female I have ever met," he said with more truth than delicacy.

Because she liked his bluntness, she favoured him with a direct reply. "I *am* odd, as you have astutely observed, but the fault is not entirely my own. You see, I was born too late. I ought to have been born in the last century. Even a decade sooner would have sufficed. In former times, a lady was permitted to achieve prominence—for charitable works, for political influence, for the number of her lovers or nameless children, for patronizing and cultivating genius. But nowadays, ladies must play a confined role. Piety is all the rage; piety which is as public and profligate as immorality was formerly. I ask you, sir, can you imagine me trying to pass in the world as pious?"

Fascinated by the outlandish opinions and the lady who professed them, the young man said, "You are compelling me to like you, when I had fully made up my mind not to. Such a turnabout is more than inconvenient; it is mortifying."

She shook a graceful gloved finger. "You are as precipitous in your liking as in your disliking. As I said earlier, you must suspend judgement of any kind for a time—a fortnight at least. At the end of that period, you shall come to me with your verdict. And to show you that I shall harbour no resentment, regardless of the outcome, I make this solemn vow: immediately following your announcement, I shall give you the honour of taking me to a play."

ASHTON'S PROGRESS towards the champagne was impeded by the scratching of lace-clad fingers on his arm. He turned round to find himself embraced by an effusion of powder.

"Oh, Tony, my dear Tony" was sniffled over and over again into his cravat.

With a finger under her plump chin, he lifted her face so that he could look into her eyes. "Dear Tassie, where have you been hiding? I thought you had made up your mind to cut me." He held her away so that he might behold her tear-streaked visage.

"I only just heard you had come," she wailed. "I sat in my little parlour waiting to hear you had arrived, but nobody ever tells me anything. I scarcely know why I consent to live with my cousin Bella when nobody in this household regards me higher than that," on which she snapped her finger in the air.

"If you had not found me, I should have found you."

She brushed away the powder she had spewed on his coat. "You ought never to have gone away, Tony," she mourned. "It was too bad of you."

"I did not go away. I was sent away."

"Yes, but you ought not to have paid that any mind. A man may be sent away, but it does not follow that he must go."

He betrayed not a shred of emotion as he replied, "When one's wife declares that she intends to elope with another man, there is not much use in staying, is there?"

"But if you had stayed, you would have seen that it all came to nothing. She never went off with him."

"Yes, so I see."

Tassie pulled a handkerchief from her puffed sleeve and wiped her nose. "You will not heed my opinion, I'm sure. No one heeds my opinion. Nevertheless, I am the only one who knows the truth of what happened—the only one, that is, besides Bella herself."

He could not resist encouraging Tassie to explain. Happily, the good woman required little encouragement to go on.

"Oh, Tony, have you not ever wondered how it was possible that Bella could have loved a man so different from you, an absolute pigeon-heart who would not say boo to a goose?"

When he half smiled at this vehement representation of his rival, Tassie coloured, saying, "You will excuse my vulgar phrase, I'm sure. No one here minds what I say."

"I find what you have to say in every way delightful."

"But there is something so dreadfully stern in your look, Tony."

He ignored this reflection, saying, "I have heard that Mattingly is dead. Is it true?"

"His dying was the only good he ever did in this world."

He acknowledged this bloodthirsty opinion with a wry laugh. "I suppose he loved Bella in his way. In any case, she loved him to distraction; she told me so."

"You know what Bella is. She will always take it into her head to love those whom no one else could possibly love. All her life she has been the soul of perversity. It is part of her charm."

"I fear you are prejudiced in my favour. Mattingly's wife evidently loved him too."

"Well, as his wife, she was obliged to love him." Suddenly, she lowered her voice to confide, "She died, too, you know, very soon after he did. I vow, she did it so that she might follow him to hell and torment him for all Eternity."

"That is not a very charitable notion," he said, "but I sincerely hope it is accurate."

"Oh, Tony, could you not forgive Bella?"

With every appearance of serenity, he said, "Of course I forgive her."

This statement brightened the good woman's face. Words of gratitude gushed forth. "Thank heaven! Then you will return to Ashton House tomorrow. I assure you, everything will be as comfortable as can be, for Bella has made the house entirely ready to receive you."

Tenderly but firmly, he answered, "No, my dearest Tassie. I have taken rooms in St. James's."

With an expression of the most complete misery, she said, "I do not see why you should take rooms when you already have a house."

He tucked her hand in his arm. "Come, you must meet my cousin Celeste. You will like her."

"I do not wish to like her," she pouted. "I do not wish to like anybody."

On that, he escorted Tassie to where Celeste awaited him. Within two minutes of their introduction, the good woman was captivated by the girl's modesty and beauty. In a whisper to Ashton, she said, "Bella said I must be kind to your cousins. What may I do to make Miss DuChateau welcome?"

"Perhaps you might engage her companion in conversation." Here he gestured towards Wild Goose, who kept her vigil by the pillar and, by her expression, defied the company to approach.

Horrified, Tassie recoiled. "What am I to say to her? I have never before addressed a savage."

"She is quite civilized. Indeed, Bella will assure you that she is a princess."

"Do you think she means to relieve me of my scalp?"

"An ill-bred savage might do so, but not a princess."

He no sooner made the introduction than he caught sight of a sumptuously dressed gentleman standing in the entryway, carrying a stick of carved ebony and looking with a sneer at all he surveyed. The new arrival wore a crimson coat cut horizontal in the waist and square in the tails. White satin breeches and white patterned stockings accented his figure. His neck was duly constricted by a whalebone high collar and a starched neckcloth of immaculate white, and he sported white gloves. Because his attire was in the highest kick of fashion and his hair short and unpowdered in the newest mode, he presented the very picture of a tulip of fashion, until one saw that the gentleman's toplofty visage was wrinkled, spotted and sagging with age.

Ashton smiled at the sight of the Old Duke. He had relished the prospect of coming face-to-face once more with Isabella's grandfather. The Duke of Wortwell had always regarded him with disdain. Ashton devoutly hoped he was in for his customary treatment, for, unlike the mild Anthony Ashton who had quit England two years before, he was now ready to give as good as he got.

CHAPTER THREE

WHEN ISABELLA SAW who had entered, she went to greet him at once. "Grandpapa, I hope you remember that you promised to behave yourself this evening."

He permitted her to buss his cheek. "No, my dear. You asked me to promise, but I never did. Now, where is this husband of yours? Did he show himself here tonight?"

"Why should he not be here? It is his house, after all."

With a noise of disgust, the Old Duke declared that the man had no other right to Ashton House but that of paying for its lease. "I never liked the fellow," he stated. "He has no blood. The Ashtons have never had any blood."

"And you have no wine, Grandpapa. Shall I fetch you a glass?"

"There is no acquiring blood, Bella, not by diligence, ambition, riches or even swindling. There is no marrying blood, either. One must be born with it. If one is not born with blood, one must accept one's inferior place in the world."

Isabella put her arm through her grandfather's and reminded him gently, "Mr. Ashton is a gentleman and the son of a gentleman."

"Ah, but where does he get his fortune? From a chandler's shop, that's where."

"It has been three centuries since the Ashtons have had anything to do with so useful an occupation as chandlery. As you well know, they have for generations led lives of unblemished idleness."

"Deuce take me, one might mistake you for a Jacobin, or, what is worse, an American. It is the influence of that fellow whom you call husband, and who, by the by, has never shown a proper reverence for the distinctions ordained by Heaven."

Thinking it wise to end this dispute, Isabella summoned a servant to fetch a chair and another to fetch a glass of wine.

The Old Duke removed a perfumed handkerchief from his coat and gracefully waved it about before dabbing his nose. "I am here to look after you, my dear. Now that your father has passed from this vale of tears, there is only myself to see to your welfare. Lord knows that cousin of yours, Tassie, hasn't the wit to do it. I do not know why you took her in to live with you. One should be charitable only at Christmas time, especially to one's poor relations. Anything more is vulgar."

"Grandpapa, I am nearly twenty-eight years of age," Isabella said, laughing. "I am perfectly capable of looking after myself."

Scandalized, he looked about to see who might have overheard the number she had uttered. "You cannot possibly be such an age," he rasped. "Why that would make me..." and here he stopped, appalled at the number which leapt to mind, though it was ten years short of what it ought to have been.

The servant came up with the chair and two other servants. Isabella induced her grandfather to sit, after which she caused him to be carried to a corner of the room where he might hold court safely out of the way.

She sent a servant to fetch a stool so that the Old
Duke's foot might be raised and his gouty toe made
comfortable. Taking a glass of wine from the footman, she handed it to the Old Duke. And, to engage
him in conversation, she beckoned to a number of female guests with reputations for pretty looks, pleasant manners and pliant morals.

Her efforts were in vain. She looked up to see Ashton approaching, his fine, square jaw set for battle. At
the sight of him, she nearly sank, for she knew that the
years elapsed had not sufficed to make either her
grandfather or her husband likely to give an inch.

Ashton greeted the duke with a crisp bow.

The Old Duke sipped daintily from his glass, over
the rim of which he fixed Ashton with a look calculated to make him duly humble. "So you have come
back, have you?"

Ashton allowed that he had.

"And I suppose you expect to take up again as you
left off, as though nothing were amiss?"

"I expect to attend to my affairs."

The Old Duke glared suspiciously. "I suppose you
expect to live in Bella's house once more?"

Isabella would have pointed out that the house be-
longed to Ashton, that everything she ate, wore or
enjoyed was, for the most part, owned by Ashton,
that, indeed, she herself was deemed by the law to be
the property of Mr. Ashton, but the man himself interrupted here to say, "I have no such expectation."

This response surprised Isabella. She had never
questioned that he would wish to live again in his own
house.

The Old Duke was surprised as well, though he
would not give Ashton the satisfaction of being delighted. On the contrary, in a tone of indignation, he

said, "Well, I suppose you expect Bella to repair at your convenience to Candover and do the pretty as hostess."

Isabella held her breath. To return with Ashton to his country estate was the first wish of her heart.

Ashton said mildly, "I would not presume to ask it of her."

Isabella had looked forward to resuming her duties as hostess, to resuming all her wifely duties. Hearing Ashton's declaration, she felt more than disappointed. She felt grieved.

The duke demanded, "Do not think that you can impose on Bella as you were used to do in former days. Oh, no, sir, for I will not have it. You have forfeited your rights as husband."

Ashton levelled a hard look at each of them. "I do not intend to claim any rights as her husband."

Bella was stung. Her impulse was to speak out then and there, to tell him that she thanked heaven he had come back, that she intended to make it up to him and that she could explain all that had happened to drive them apart, but her grandfather intervened.

"Then you will continue to live apart from Bella and refrain from imposing on her good nature by making a nuisance of yourself."

"I shall inform you of my intentions," Ashton said, "as soon as I have informed Bella, and not before." On that, he favoured them with an elegant bow and rejoined Miss DuChateau.

The Old Duke stared at the spot where Ashton had stood. Then, with an effort, he turned to regard Isabella. His face appeared white under his rouge. "Insolent puppy," he muttered.

Isabella did not hear, for she was rapt in listening to the sound of her own breathing. Dread overtook her as she reviewed what she had just heard: Ashton did not intend to live with her or take her to Candover or assert any of his husbandly rights. Although she longed to know what he did intend, she was almost afraid to know. This Anthony Ashton was no longer the husband who had sailed to the New World. He was not the man she had dreamed would return to her. Nor was he the man she had met and fallen in love with at a London ball in what now seemed the most sublime Season of her life.

IN THE SUMMER of her twenty-second year, by which time her family had despaired of her ever marrying, Isabella had gone to a private assembly and was standing among a group of admirers when all at once a scorching sensation suffused her back. Slowly, so that she would attract no notice, she shifted her position so as to see who stood behind her. It turned out to be a handsome, imposing, half-smiling gentleman who looked at her with burning eyes.

Since her debut, Isabella had had a surfeit of lovesick glances aimed her way. They were distinguished by a certain spaniel droop about the mouth, a lunatic glaze of the eye, and a sighing from the bosom which put her strongly in mind of an old creaking chair. But this gentleman's look froze and melted her at the same time. It was starkly, openly and unapologetically passionate. What saved it from an excess of sentiment was its irony, as though the gentleman was amused by the nakedness of his own feeling. Her first thought was that he must be mad, her next that he looked at her the way she had longed to be looked at.

He approached her, and without taking his eyes from hers, addressed the host and begged the honour of an introduction. The gentleman must have granted the wish, for she found her hand in Mr. Anthony Ashton's as he led her down the line of dancers.

After dancing several turns, she said, "If you continue to look at me in that manner, sir, you will set the ballroom on fire, which is sure to kick up a scandal."

He smiled. "And nothing terrifies you so much as scandal."

"It is mother's milk to me."

"So I have heard."

"Oh, you have heard some gossip? Tell me what it is. I love to hear what they are saying of me. Did they tell you I am an accomplished flirt?"

"Yes, but I did not have to hear any gossip. I made enquiries."

She swallowed, then did what she had not done since the age of seven: she blushed.

He appeared to derive much satisfaction from this response.

"You had seen me before?"

"I saw you at Pimlico. When you won, you threw your arms about the pony, then went about demanding that your bets be paid on the spot."

"Well, what did you learn by your enquiries?" she asked a little breathlessly.

"That you are unpredictable, intelligent, interesting. They did not have to tell me you were beautiful."

"You make me out a paragon. I assure you, I am not."

"I forgot to add your principal attraction, namely, that you do not feed on flattery."

"Nobody could possibly have spoken so much good of me, not in London at any rate."

"No, they told me you were accounted a flirt, that you had jilted an army of unexceptionable gentlemen and that your opinions were quite shocking. The truth of your character I was forced to deduce myself.''

''It may be that you have given me a better character than I deserve, that their disapproving estimations are accurate.''

''Yes, that is why I have determined to find out for myself.''

She liked him the better for not seizing that opportunity to shower her with compliments.

He had called at the earliest possible moment on the following day, haunted her father's house for the next six days, and then, as they took the air along Rotten Row, he asked her to marry him.

She looked at him as though he were raving. ''You are not serious. You are merely treating me to a taste of that irony by which I have come to know you.''

His cheek came dangerously close to hers. ''Put me to the test.''

''You scarcely know me. You certainly do not know any good of me.''

''I know that I cannot get enough of you.''

His ardour made her feel what she had never felt before: shy. The shyness was intensified by the powerful attraction she felt to this man. An instinct urged her to give in to the feeling, but her reason warned her not to take him at his word, for if she did, she might fall in love with him; if she fell in love with him, she would come to depend upon him; and if she came to depend upon him, or anybody for that matter, she would be done for.

As she could find the voice neither to accept nor refuse him, he approached her father, who was not only willing but eager to give his daughter to a gentleman who demanded no dowry and was prepared to be more than generous to his father-in-law. The knowledge that

the Old Duke would be furious if his granddaughter
did not marry into the nobility spurred him to close the
transaction. When the settlements were agreed upon,
Anthony Ashton came to Isabella asking her again to
have him.

"This is rash, reckless," she cried. "I know less
than nothing of being mistress of a country estate, of
overseeing servants and a bakehouse, of visiting the
sick and getting up baskets for the poor."

"The housekeeper will do up the baskets, I promise you."

"My talents lie in dancing and flirting. If you marry
me, you will live in a ramshackle household. The servants will steal the plate and the cook will swill gin."

"You would not wish to spare me such misery if you
did not love me to distraction."

As he had just described her feelings with perfect
precision, she could not meet his eyes, let alone reply.

He put his hands to her cheeks and said simply, "I
love you, Bella, and I do not need servants and cooks
to make me happy. I need you." Then he kissed her,
an insistent, demanding kiss, and, in spite of herself,
she was done for.

ABRUPTLY, Isabella was recalled from these memories by Tassie, who brought forward Wild Goose to
meet the Old Duke. Shaking off the effect of the rem-
iniscence, she steeled herself for what was yet to come.
She saw the duke behold in horror the Indian's attire
and coiffure, and she could not help but sigh to think
what manner of snub her grandfather was contem-
plating.

But as soon as he heard her title, the duke struggled to his feet with the help of a footman and intoned, "Your Royal Highness."

In her turn, Wild Goose looked the Old Duke up and down, grimaced as though she smelled a three-day fish and declared, "Sick man eat turnip!"

Tassie gasped.

Isabella, who knew her grandfather scorned to eat anything so lowly as a turnip, laughed.

After a moment's pause, the duke allowed that he was very ill indeed and none but the daughter of a great and noble house would have evinced such acuity and sensitivity upon first meeting. If they might be permitted to sit, he said, he should be happy to hear the princess elucidate upon her receipt for good health.

After they had seated themselves, Wild Goose snatched the wine from the Old Duke's hand and handed it to a footman. From a pouch which hung on her sash, she took what appeared to be a small desiccated carrot. "Turnip," she said, handing it to the duke, who blanched. Gravely, she sat by his side and would not be content until the gentleman had consumed every bit of the medicinal wonder.

It pleased Isabella to see that her grandfather had met his match in wilfulness. Knowing he would be well entertained, she inhaled a breath for courage and went in search of her husband.

As soon as he spied her crossing the room, Ashton recognized the look of purpose on her face. He stood outside the circle of dancers, waiting to meet her. When she reached him, she opened her mouth to speak and stopped. The eyes of her guests, even those who were dancing, were again riveted on them. Everywhere she looked, she was observed. Tears filled her eyes. Those tears, which bespoke vexation at herself for inviting the stares of the world, were not lost on Ashton.

Wordlessly, he put his hand on her waist and guided her into the line of waltzers.

She gave him a grateful look.

They danced a moment, their eyes locked—whether in combat or fascination the onlookers could not say—and then he swept her along the circle with an energy which caused Isabella to catch her breath. She drew as close to him as she dared, feeling the strength of his presence.

As he manoeuvered her round a turn, his cheek brushing her hair, he breathed in the fragrance of lily of the valley. With the next turn, his hand moved from her waist to her bare back.

Feeling his touch on her skin, Isabella shivered.

The sensation of her trembling beneath his hand alerted him. He slowed their dancing, moved an inch away, and said coolly, "Bella, we have a matter of business to discuss."

"Excellent. I adore business." She endeavoured to make her voice as light as the violins they danced to. "When you left London, I daresay nothing could have been better guaranteed to make me run from a room shrieking in terror than the threat of taking up business. But I have reformed my ways, as you shall see. Now I embrace every opportunity to discuss tiresome matters, and when one presents itself, I am in positive raptures." Her emotion quickened her breathing.

"The matter of business I must put before you is not pleasant."

"A little gloom merely adds spice," she said, with more hope than conviction.

"The ballroom is not a fitting place to discuss the matter. I should like to call on you tomorrow."

"I should like you to call, of course, but you need not check your conversation simply because we are dancing. I find no place more conducive to serious business than a ballroom. Tell me what this matter is which causes you to furrow your brow and look so black.''

''It would be best to wait. It will keep until tomorrow.''

''If you do not tell me this instant, I shall inform Wild Goose and she will make you eat a turnip.'' She gave him a brilliant smile, wondering what lengths she would have to go to in order to win a smile in return.

He eyed her gravely. ''Bella, you are far too fond of having your own way. You shall be sorry for it.''

His sternness chilled her. Recklessly, she said, ''You need not be so mysterious about this matter of business, Tony. As it happens, I believe I know what you wish to discuss. It is marriage, is it not? I assure you, I am ready to discuss it this very instant.''

''Ah, you wish to discuss marriage, do you? I cannot recall your ever evincing much interest in the subject before.''

She coloured. ''Such a rich subject, matrimony. I believe there cannot be too much said about it.''

He did not take up her gay tone. His look was severe. ''It is not precisely marriage I wish to discuss, Bella.''

''Not marriage? What then, my dear husband?''

''In point of fact, my dear wife,'' he said, ''it is divorce.''

CHAPTER FOUR

WHEN THE GUESTS HAD GONE home, Isabella, along with Tassie and a half-finished bottle of champagne, repaired to Bella's upstairs sitting-room. The moment they entered this favourite parlour, where a welcoming fire had been lit, they heard the watch call out the hour of four. Tassie took a chair by the fender. Isabella, wearied from smiling, joking and pretending to have not a care in the world, sank onto a sofa. She had not permitted herself more than a sip of wine while the rigours of the evening required her unflagging vigilance. Now she drank a glass of champagne and told herself that it was merely the bubbles which stung her eyes.

Tassie complained, "You did not send the footman to tell me that Tony had come."

"Forgive me. In all the flutter of meeting my husband, I quite forgot."

"Naturally, you forgot. I am nothing. Nobody regards me."

Isabella poured her cousin a glass and brought it to her. "Dear Tassie, I do mind you, for you have been my true friend through everything. Here is your reward," she said and handed her the glass. After she kicked off her slippers and set them near the hearth, she resumed her pensive position on the sofa.

Tassie drained the glass in one draught. Much refreshed, she said, "I was very much your friend tonight. I no sooner set eyes on Tony than I told him he must come back to us in Hertford Street.''

Isabella sat up. "You did what?''

"Oh, yes, and I gave him my opinion of Philip Mattingly.''

"Tassie, you took your oath you would never breathe a word.''

"I did not break my oath. I merely gave a hint, so that you may go to him with the truth without further delay.''

"I cannot do that.''

Tassie stood like a shot. "But you have been praying for this opportunity from the moment he left England.''

"You must promise me never to say another word to him on this subject.''

"I will give no such promise. It is folly.''

"When have you ever known me to avoid a thing merely because it was folly?''

"Be serious, Bella.''

"I am perfectly serious. There is no use in speaking to him. Tony wishes to divorce me. He told me so tonight.''

Shocked silence followed this announcement. Unsteadily, Tassie lowered herself into her chair. Then, shaking her head dazedly, she said weakly, "I don't believe it.''

"You will oblige me by not disputing what I have heard from Tony's own lips. I have scarcely absorbed the fact myself.''

"What did you say when he told you?''

"I do not recall. I felt numb, wholly at a loss. I babbled something; it scarcely matters. What does one say to such an announcement?''

"Do you mean to stand there like a lump and allow such a thing to happen? Go to him at once and tell him everything. Tell him you never loved Mattingly. Tell him it was merely one of your schemes. I shall have Weeks fetch the carriage. Tony will not mind being wakened in the dead of night to hear such news."

Brushing a streak of wet from her cheek, Isabella said, "He will never believe me. He will think my explanation merely a ruse to prevent the divorce."

"He could not be so cruel as to doubt you."

"What is to prevent his thinking I am lying now as I lied then? How am I to convince him?"

As the impossibility of the situation burst upon her, Tassie put her head in her hands. "We must do something, Bella. It is no longer the fashion to be divorced. Indeed, there are those who will shun you once the decree is made, who will expect you to shut yourself away from all Society and spend the rest of your life in contemplation and atonement."

The notion that she could lead such an upright life revived Isabella's sense of the absurd, so that she laughed through wet eyes. "How very charming!" she exclaimed. "You know I have always wished for simplicity and solitude, eking out a living on the little I might cultivate by my own hand—I am so very fond of gardening. I am sure I should adore living the life of a recluse in the country—in Cornwall, perhaps; yes, it shall be Cornwall. We shall shear sheep and pick berries, or pick sheep and shear berries, whichever it is."

"You'll sing a different tune when we are forced to remove from this house into a hovel and to wear rags and push barrows!"

"But think how happy we shall be. Why, here in Hertford Street we must look for ways to quarrel with our situation. Once we are exiled, we shall have no end of reasons to complain."

"We shall be destitute. Nothing is so tedious as being poor."

Isabella sighed. "Grandpapa will not let us starve. It will give him great pleasure to put us on an allowance and then throw his generosity in our teeth."

Tassie rose and came to her. Urgently, she said, "If you cannot tell Tony, permit me to go to him for you."

"What is the use? It is clear he does not love me. The only sensible thing is to allow him to be free of me with as little inconvenience as possible."

"For shame, Bella. How can you talk so? Have you no morals?"

"No, not a great many," Isabella said, subdued. "That is why Tony is divorcing me, I expect."

Beside herself, Tassie cried, "I wish you would not speak of yourself in that manner. You know very well you are not nearly as wicked as you like everyone to think. You are merely wilful, perverse and difficult."

"It is true that I never permitted Philip to touch my heart or my person, but I did behave wickedly, Tassie, very wickedly. I schemed and tricked and lied, thinking that if I made Tony believe I was in love with Philip, I would draw him to me again. Instead, I drove him to put an ocean between us. I can never forget it as long as I live."

Tassie threw her handkerchief over her face and wept. "We shall end in a sponging house."

"Poor Tassie. I am afraid there must be a vast deal more trouble before it is all over, and it is all my fault."

"Your grandfather will blame me. He does not like me."

Bella took out her linen and wiped a streak of tears from her cousin's cheek. Gently, she whispered, "He does not like anybody, so think nothing of it. Besides, when have you ever known me to do the sensible thing? For that matter, when have you ever known me to make life convenient for Tony?"

Tassie looked up and blinked at her.

"What I am trying to tell you," Bella said with a sorrowful smile, "is that in spite of all I have said, I am compelled to do what I can to change Tony's mind."

In her ecstasy, Tassie snatched the linen from Bella's hand and waved it about. "Bella, I knew you could not be so foolish as to be divorced!"

Unable to share her cousin's ecstasy, Isabella asked, "But what if I should fail? How will you bear it? How will *I* bear it?"

"You cannot fail. He loved you more than any man ever loved a woman. A man does not soon recover from that sort of passion, any more than he may soon recover from the plague."

Isabella could not help raising her brows. "I thank you for the compliment. It is not often I am compared to a case of the plague. Unfortunately, Mr. Anthony Ashton is no longer the man I married. He is hard. I confess he frightens me a little. Moreover, he may have his choice of wives. He may choose for himself one with everything to recommend her: youth, beauty, modesty, breeding, charm, affection, wealth— not to mention loyalty."

"Nonsense. Such a creature cannot exist, and if she did, Tony must think her tiresome compared with you."

Isabella laughed. "With you by my side, Tassie, there is no danger of my ever growing conceited."

"Oh, you do not mind what I say. Nobody does."

"But I do mind it, for I sincerely hope you are right and that Tony has no desire to be married to the sort of woman he deserves. In the meantime, I must induce him to forget his dislike of me and make him love me again. The question is, how on Earth am I to do it?"

"You will find a way, Bella. You will think of just the right stratagem."

"It was stratagems which put me in this dreadful case to begin with."

Kissing her cousin's plump, powdered cheek, she rose and went to warm her toes near the fire, the better to think, while Tassie was left to contemplate with a shudder the prospect of Cornwall and sheep.

WHEN TASSIE LEFT HER, Isabella, who was not sleepy, took up a piece of half-finished work. As she stitched, she recollected Tony's announcement and the numbing impact it had had on her. She had expected, when she saw him, that his characteristic irony would cloak deep anger and, accordingly, had fortified herself. But never in her wildest dreams had she anticipated divorce. The ladies and gentlemen of her set had always been content to remain married regardless of how much they detested each other. They lived, very agreeably, in their estimation, according to an arrangement by which either spouse might enjoy any number of liaisons and produce any number of by-blows. In this manner the aristocracy had rendered divorce unnecessary. It was not a system conducive to either happy or sensible living, in Isabella's view, but it had one thing to recommend it: it was neither so extreme nor so final as divorce.

For him to go to all the trouble of divorcing her, she knew, Tony's resentment must go even deeper than she had imagined, and that knowledge filled her with the profoundest remorse. She wished she might do precisely as Tassie had urged: go to him with the truth and have done with pretense and scheming, but it was too late for plain-speaking. He would think her confession merely a plot to prevent the divorce, and he would be right, except that she would have meant every word.

For a moment, she despaired. It was inconceivable, she felt, that she could possess the power of renewing his love. How could a man continue an attachment to a wife who had treated him abominably, who had told him to his face that she meant to put herself under the protection of another man? Yet she had no choice but to make the attempt—not because she feared disgrace, exile or penury, as Tassie did, but because she had fallen in love with him the night he had scorched her back with his eyes and had never stopped loving him, nor ever would.

AFTER DEPOSITING his cousins at the house he had taken for them in Upper Berkeley Street, Ashton returned to his hotel. Too restless for sleep, he left his rooms and walked the damp streets, reviewing the events of the evening. His meeting with Isabella had produced a more powerful effect than he had anticipated, and he now wished to sort out the nature of that effect.

Looking up, he noticed that he had walked as far as Hertford Street. He was too near Ashton House, he decided, not to have another look at it, and when in a few moments he stood before it, he could see that it was singularly elegant, like its occupant. Pretty white-framed windows on each of the four stories lent it a symmetrical appearance. Its black door was framed by two simple Doric columns. The gargoyle door-knocker he and Bella had purchased during their honeymoon gleamed at him in the moonlight. Isabella would have liked a flower garden, he recollected, but there was no having such luxury where vertical living at close quarters with one's neighbours was the fashion.

Everything about the house was just as he remembered it, except that it was smaller. Having grown accustomed to the grandeur of Canada's blue, snow-covered peaks, vast lakes and rushing streams, he now viewed England in a different proportion. He did not value its beauties the less, but he saw them with greater clarity. When he had left England, he had seen nothing but his own disappointment and betrayal. That view had changed the instant he had arrived in Ontario.

There he had let it be known that he was on the lookout for adventure, and that character had recommended him warmly to Mr. Gerald DuChateau's acquaintance. That gentleman opened his heart and home to the stranger, and as Ashton had for some time experienced a staggering loneliness, he gladly accepted this hospitality. The family DuChateau treated him as fondly as though he were another son. Soon Guy came to think of him as a brother. When they discovered to their mutual pleasure that they shared a common relation who had settled in the New World in the previous century, they took to calling one another cousin, though the connection was so remote as to permit either side to ignore it if they had so chosen.

On Celeste's return from school in Switzerland, Ashton instantly acquired a sister. Her presence en-

livened her parents' household immeasurably, for they
had sorely missed the delicate, good-hearted girl who
was, with her brother, the treasure of their hearts. The
young lady's charm affected Ashton, too. Her gentleness worked a change in him. He became aware of
how much he missed a feminine presence in his life,
and he began to think that the emptiness he felt might
be filled by this young girl. Honour prevented him
from speaking to her of his growing admiration; nor
could he speak to her parents, not while he was en-
cumbered with a wife in England. Still, his imagination fixed more and more strongly on Celeste: her
beauty, her modesty, docility, eagerness, kindness and
sincerity. Best of all, she possessed the quality he most
esteemed in a female: she was as unlike Bella as it was
possible to be.

Whereas before he had kept his new friends ignorant of his full history, he now revealed to them that
he was married. The family had always sensed that
some sorrow weighed on his heart. When they learned
of his marriage, they connected it with his secret grief
and were not surprised when he announced that he
meant to return to England. The announcement delighted his cousins, for they wished to accompany him.
They hinted and cajoled until he was made to understand how important it was that Celeste be allowed to
wear a white dress and dance at a London ball and
that Guy have the opportunity to discover whether the
beauty of the English damsels was as bewitching as it
was reputed to be. To prove the earnestness of their
wishes, they went so far as to endure lessons with an
English dancing master, who taught them to perform
the mazurka and the reel in a manner guaranteed not
to absolutely disgrace them.

Ashton was pleased to grant their wish. Their companionship had ever been a solace to him. He therefore lost no time in asking Wild Goose, the family's intimate acquaintance, to attend Miss DuChateau. Gathering her herbs, beads and wampum, Wild Goose had set forth with them for England, where her task was to inspect the scores of gentlemen who were certain to ask Celeste to share their blankets. Ashton was sensible that Mr. and Mrs. DuChateau required assurance that their daughter would be protected from the wiles and snares of the London dandies, and whatever protective offices Wild Goose could not perform, he promised he would be more than happy to fulfil himself.

From these pleasant recollections, Ashton's mind drifted to his meeting with Bella, and as he mused, his smile turned caustic. He had not planned to tell her of his intentions regarding the divorce until he had had ample time to approach his solicitor and inaugurate the necessary procedures. But when she had cajoled him, when she had insisted and teased and joked, as though marriage were no more to her than a pimple on the nose of a flea, he wished to make her regret her insouciance. And so he had told her, as directly and baldly as she seemed to wish.

To his disappointment, she had betrayed scarcely any emotion. She had kept perfectly still for a long moment, then laughed and congratulated him on handing her such a prodigious surprise. Their acquaintance would be all amazement to hear the tit-bit, she had declared. Of course, nothing delighted her so much as providing amusement to lighten their impoverished lives. She had gone on at some length in that vein, so that if there had lingered in his mind any question of her indifference, it had been put to rest.

Although he despised hysterics in females, along with fits of the vapours, fainting spells and other tokens of delicacy, he would have liked it better if Bella had fallen, swooning, to the floor. He would have liked it better if she had threatened to scratch his eyes out, or even hit him. He would have liked it better if she had uttered even the faintest protest. He seethed at her complaisance. But, when at last reason overcame his irritation, he saw that her complaisance had this advantage: it strengthened his resolve to marry his young cousin as soon as Parliament should see fit to make him eligible once more.

CHAPTER FIVE

THE FOLLOWING DAY, when he called in Hertford Street, Ashton was surprised to learn that Isabella had gone out. He had told her when they had parted the evening before that he meant to call, and as the business they had to discuss was not the sort which was likely to slip one's mind, he did not think she could have forgotten. Despite this logic, however, he received repeated assurances that Mrs. Ashton was not at home.

He was strolling down Piccadilly, still puzzling over Isabella's absence, when, in front of The Egyptian Hall, amid the noise and traffic, he saw a sumptuous ebony carriage. He felt an odd jog of memory at the sight of that polished equipage, which he recognized by the coat of arms emblazoned on its door and the livery of its footmen as belonging to the Duke of Wortwell. Because the carriage blocked his view, he could not see the passenger alight, but he thought it might be Isabella, for in the past, the Old Duke had liked to spoil her by putting his carriage at her disposal.

All at once the carriage pulled away and he saw Isabella, dressed in a burgundy pelisse, white skirt and feathered bonnet. He would have approached but she was engaged in animated conversation with a blade of the Town. Bella had ever been a great favourite with the gentlemen, he knew, and seeing her with an admirer suddenly dispelled his earlier puzzlement. Now it was clear, he thought grimly, why she had been out when he had called in Hertford Street.

He meant to hail a hack and waste no further time in the precincts of Piccadilly, but at that moment, the dandy bowed and took leave of Isabella. A moment later, Ashton saw her turn and enter Hatchard's, quite alone.

Immediately he crossed the street and followed her into the bookstore, meaning to intercept her and take her by surprise. Inside the shop, he saw her engaged in conversation with an acquaintance, Lady Pillowbank, a talkative female with whom he had renewed his acquaintance the previous evening in Bella's ballroom and whom he had no great desire to meet again. The two women were sufficiently rapt in what they were saying as to allow him to enter the shop unseen.

He availed himself of a chair near a neat row of shelves and, awaiting an opportunity to present himself to Isabella, took up a broadsheet which lay on a table. From that vantage point, he could scarcely avoid overhearing Isabella's conversation. He heard Lady Pillowbank cry, "My dear Bella, if it is a book you are after, you must permit me to advise you. I am a prodigious reader and my taste is famous, I assure you."

"As my own taste is infamous," Isabella replied, "I shall put myself entirely in your hands."

"A wise decision. Now, what will suit you best? I have it! You must read something elevating—perhaps a treatise on the picturesque."

Ashton could hear the archness in Isabella's voice as she said, "Do you really think it proper for a female to know how to distinguish the picturesque from the merely beautiful?"

"Indeed I do!" cried her ladyship in all serious-
ness. "Why, every female ought to be able to understand the delights of Nature's handiwork. Such a study
will infuse her with ardent patriotism. She will learn
that English scenery is the most picturesque in all the
world."

"But what of Canada? I am told that it, too, boasts
a vast deal of scenery."

"Regardless of place, a treatise on the picturesque
must be advantageous, for it will improve a lady's
conversation. To be able to converse on the picturesque is to be valuable to any hostess."

"I should be pleased to be valuable to somebody.
Therefore, the picturesque it shall be, by all means."

Ashton settled back in his chair, prepared to enjoy
the sound of Isabella's quizzing.

"While you are selecting a treatise on the picturesque," Isabella added, "perhaps you would be good
enough to recommend a book on the subject of matrimony."

At that reference, Ashton sat forward, all curious
attention.

Lady Pillowbank laughed conspiratorially. "I understand, my dear. Now your charming Ashton is returned, you must find a way to keep him here."

To his infinite irritation, he could not make out
what Bella said in reply or if she said anything at all.
He endeavoured to listen more closely.

"Well, for matrimony," her ladyship said, "you
must go to Gisborne. Whenever Lord Pillowbank
takes it into his head to have his own way about a
thing, I immediately consult my Gisborne, for he
teaches that a wife's duty is never to let her husband
do as he wishes but only what is proper."

"I'm afraid I do not possess any talent for what Mr. Gisborne recommends. A woman who cannot do what is proper herself can hardly insist that her husband do so."

"Nonsense! I shall ask the bookseller to find you a copy of *An Enquiry into the Duties of the Female Sex,* a most excellent work of its kind." On that, she went in search of the bookseller.

Ashton felt that he might now rise to greet Isabella. He promised himself delicious satisfaction in the astonishment he was about to inspire, but her lady-ship immediately returned with a copy of Gisborne, causing him to sit down again. After showing off the volume's binding and paper, she took the liberty of reading aloud from one of its cut pages:

Wealth may be secured, rank may be obtained; but if wealth and rank are to be the main ingre-dients in the cup of matrimonial felicity, the sweetness of wine will be exhausted at once, and nothing remain but bitter and corrosive dregs.

"Gracious me!" Isabella declared with exagger-ated amazement, "your Mr. Gisborne has been scrib-bling about me. I should like to know precisely how he has learned of my history."

Baffled, Lady Pillowbank replied, "I do not think he was referring to you, my dear. He was speaking in a general way."

"I do not see how he could speak of drinking sweet wine without having spied upon me; I am partial to sweet wine, as all the world knows full well. Nor could he make such pathetic reference to 'bitter and corro-sive dregs' without knowing of my grandfather's cellar, which was always renowned for being the worst in all Europe.''

Isabella's humour was lost on the lady but not on Ashton. It had been a very long time since he had been moved to laugh as she made him laugh.

Lady Pillowbank argued, "Mr. Gisborne leads a reclusive life and rarely comes to Town. He is unlikely to have heard of you.''

"Are you suggesting," said Isabella in an offended tone, "that my reputation does not extend beyond London?''

Her ladyship hastened to contradict such a notion. "I don't mean to say that at all. Your reputation is known everywhere, even abroad, I daresay. Why, now I think of it, I suppose it is possible that Mr. Gisborne knows something of your history, for his warnings in regard to rank and wealth might well refer to the circumstances of your marriage to Mr. Ashton.''

Ashton smiled wryly as it occurred to him that those who eavesdrop are always punished by hearing themselves spoken of.

"All the world knows," Lady Pillowbank went on, "that your father, though youngest son of a duke, was heel over ears in debt, and that he married you to Simon Ashton's son in exchange for fifteen thousand pounds.''

"Oh, it must have been at least sixteen thousand, very likely more," Isabella responded, laughing. "The granddaughter of a duke does not go for a farthing less than sixteen. I am mortified to hear that the gossips have set my price at fifteen.''

Ashton saw that the intimate details of his life were common knowledge in London. Though public notoriety was not greatly to his taste, he was amused to think how much entertainment he and Bella supplied the gossips of the Town.

"Regardless of the figure, it is well known that it was your father's connections and Mr. Ashton's wealth which secured the union."

"I am always charmed to hear what amazing opinions the world conceives, but the truth is much more interesting. You see, my father had quarrelled with his father and refused to grant him the privilege of paying off his debts. Instead, he married me to an Ashton in exchange for a vast deal of money. The world may think the exchange was made for the sake of prudence, but the true motive was spite. My father wished to disoblige his father, as Grandpapa had disobliged his father before him, and his father before him, and so on since the beginning of time."

"That is as may be, my dear, but it was afterwards agreed everywhere that it was a love match."

"A love match," Isabella repeated quietly.

Intently, Ashton listened for more, but she said nothing further. He wondered what had made her pause over the words, and why, suddenly, she had no sparkling rejoinder ready to hand.

"Oh, yes, it was known everywhere that he was quite wildly in love with you and you with him, which was fortunate because Mr. Gisborne entirely approves of love matches, where there is money to permit them, of course."

Ashton waited to hear Isabella's response. More than likely, he thought, she would answer with her customary wit. She might even deny that their union had been a love match, dismissing it as a mere escapade. There was a leaden moment, empty of sound, and then he heard Isabella remark in an uncharacteristically agitated tone, "Mr. Gisborne may regard love matches highly, but, oh, Lady Pillowbank, they can be hard, very hard."

Ashton sat back. He had given over expecting sensibility from Bella. He could not be certain, but the tenor of her words sounded to him very like regret.

"Surely you believe that love can conquer all," Lady Pillowbank said. "You have proved as much, have you not?"

Again, Ashton heard a heavy silence. Then, with a lightness he thought strained, Isabella replied, "Well, I am reassured to know that my history supplies food for speculation. After all, what is the use of leading a life if no one talks of it? I bear Mr. Gisborne no ill will for mentioning me in his book. I shall take it home with me this instant."

He heard the two women walk to another part of the shop, and while the books were being wrapped and tied into a neat parcel for Isabella, he noiselessly left the shop.

In the street stood a hack, waiting for a passenger. The driver looked his way and tipped his hat. "Hack, sir?" he invited.

Ashton declined. A hack was the last thing he wanted. The moment was too ripe for him to drive off. He had heard much to pique his curiosity during the past quarter hour, and taken all in all, it suggested that Bella might not be as impervious to emotion as he had thought—or as she had wished him to think. He wanted to hear more, and he wanted to see more—her expressions, gestures, movements and the light in her green eyes. Isabella had indulged her wit by quizzing poor Lady Pillowbank. Now, he promised himself, it was her turn to be teased.

PART TWO

The Face of One's Enemy

CHAPTER SIX

ISABELLA COLLIDED with a gentleman on her way to the door. As soon as she saw who it was, she blushed and scolded herself for blushing. His complete ease increased her discomfort. Happily, Lady Pillowbank seized the offices of conversation. "My dear Ashton," she cooed, "how glad you must be to be home again."

"You have kept England in very good condition while I was away," he said, removing his hat. "I thank you, my lady."

"By 'home again,' I meant Ashton House, of course. After sleeping in mud holes and such you must be vastly pleased to be able to rest your head on a proper pillow. I daresay I never catch a wink of sleep unless I am in my own bed."

At this allusion, Isabella glanced swiftly at Ashton and saw that he regarded her with an ironic expression. By way of soothing her own apprehension, she said, "Your ladyship cannot think that Mr. Ashton has returned to England merely to sleep. Oh, no, he has important business to tend to."

"Has he? Well, Bella, you must consult your Gisborne on that head. He will advise you on the proper way to conduct your husband's business."

"Gisborne?" Ashton said as though he vaguely recollected the name. "Is he not that noble genius who writes on the subject of matrimony? Such a rich subject, matrimony. I believe there cannot be too much written about it."

Isabella shot him a look. There was nothing she detested more than hearing herself quoted. Ashton knew it, and she knew that he knew it.

Her ladyship said in a voice dripping with implication, "Isabella means to take the Gisborne home with her. I trust you will both profit from the result." On that, she bade them goodbye and went out the door in a flurry of muslin and feathers.

Isabella followed her ladyship outside. To her dismay, Ashton kept close by her side. They stood together and waved Lady Pillowbank off in her carriage.

"I called on you this morning, as promised, and found you had gone out," he said.

Isabella took a step away. "I did not think you still meant to come. What more can there possibly be to say?"

"Perhaps you wish to avoid it, whatever it is."

Her pride demanded that he not know how close he had come to the truth. "If you will look there, you will see my grandfather's carriage, ready to take me back to Hertford Street. Yet instead of allowing you to hand me inside, I stand here allowing you to quiz me. Does that sound like avoidance?"

"Well, no matter. By fortunate coincidence, I have met you in Hatchard's. How pleasant the day is," he added, looking round at the dust kicked up by the noisy traffic. "It is far too pleasant to spend indoors. Do you like to walk? You may send the carriage away if you do not wish to keep the horses standing. I shall take you home in a hack."

Taking a breath, she agreed. If she was going to succeed in her plan to make him love her again, she might as well begin now.

When the coachman drove off, Ashton proffered his arm and they walked in the direction of Green Park. As they made their way slowly along Piccadilly, they passed a governess herding a trio of children, a juggler, many pairs of shoppers, footmen on errands, ladies attended by their maids, gentlemen coming from or going to their coffee-houses, and every one of them in a great hurry. The noise and bustle gave Isabella time to ransack her well-stocked arsenal of conversation for a subject. So many subjects threatened to stir painful memories that she had to forage long and arduously. At last, she considered it safe to remark, "How delighted I was to meet your cousins."

"They were delighted to meet you, also."

"You need not try to spare me, Tony. I am well aware that Mr. DuChateau has taken me in dislike."

"You will charm him soon enough, I have no doubt."

Feeling his irony like cold water on her cheeks, she walked on with him in silence. They entered the park, where they passed among rows of elms and beeches along the Queen's Walk.

"Apart from his rude, unjust, hateful conduct towards me," she said, "I quite liked Mr. DuChateau."

"I thought you would."

"He is handsome and has a definite air. The ladies will admire him greatly, once you send your tailor and bootmaker to do something about his style."

"You find him handsome, do you?"

"Yes. I imagine he looks as you did at one-and-twenty."

"And what is your opinion of my other cousin?"

She smiled, genuinely gratified to express herself on this subject. "Miss DuChateau seems quite perfect."

He nodded. "She is."

Isabella felt relieved to have said the right thing. She could not recall when she had been so desirous of pleasing or so certain of offending. The difficulty was, she acknowledged to herself, that she was unused to the effort. She had spent a lifetime engaged in amusing, quizzing, joking and shocking, but rarely in trying to please. She had never been obliged to try to please anyone except herself. To bolster her late success, she said, "Yes, Miss DuChateau is a most delightful child."

He stared at her. "Child!"

Seeing that she had vexed him, she said in alarm, "I meant nothing against her. She is charming. It is only that she seems so very innocent, so unused to Society. But that is the most natural thing in the world, given her origins and education."

"Miss DuChateau is seventeen," he said between his teeth. "A great many girls are already married by the time they have reached that age."

"Yes, you are quite right. You will hear no argument from me there. Of course, you always used to say it was a great pity in some cases to see a girl married so very young, especially where she is foolish and wilful and ignorant of her own heart."

"Miss DuChateau is none of those, I assure you," he responded icily. "She is possessed of good sense which is often lacking in women twice her age. A child, indeed!"

Appalled at herself for having irritated him, Isabella now wished to let the matter drop. Once again, she searched her mind for an unexceptionable topic of conversation.

Before she could devise one, Ashton said, "So you have bought a copy of Gisborne, have you? An odd choice. I do not recall your ever reading the work of divines and other purveyors of sage advice."

She felt conscious and said hastily, "Oh, it is not for myself. What use could I possibly have for such a volume?"

"I see. It is a gift, then?"

"Yes, a gift," she lied, thinking that if she could utter pleasantries as easily as she uttered falsehoods, she would be well on her way to winning at least one smile from her husband.

"I confess, I am curious to know which member of your set would consent to use such a gift for anything but a doorstop."

Colouring, she said, "Oh, she is not a member of my set."

"Not a member of your set? Who is she, then? I cannot help but be curious."

Isabella cast about her for an answer. "Well, she is a member of a different set," she said lamely.

His face came near to hers as he said, "I smoke it. You wish to conceal her identity. For some reason, some scandalous reason no doubt, you feel obliged to protect the lady's reputation, which might be damaged should she be caught reading such a work."

"There is nothing scandalous about it," Isabella said, provoked. "I assure you, the lady is above reproach." She met his eyes with a challenge.

"Is she, indeed? I should like to meet this excellent creature."

"When you hear the name of the lady, you shall be sorry you ever tweaked me on the subject."

"By all means, Bella, prove me wrong. I should like nothing better. Tell me her name. Who is this mysterious creature?" He folded his arms and waited.

She looked about her, at the Doric temple in front of which they had paused, at the daffodils which bobbed at their feet, at the pale blue sky and leafing trees, at a lady and gentleman who passed by, engrossed in intimate conversation. "You wish me to tell you her name?" she said, thinking frantically.

"I can scarcely contain my anticipation, I assure you."

"Very well," she replied staunchly, "I shall tell you."

After a considerable time passed in silence, he said, "Were you intending to tell me before nightfall? I do not mean to hurry you, Bella, but I am promised to dine at ten."

"I intend to tell you this minute," she snapped. After a breath, she plunged forth. "Her name is Celeste DuChateau!"

He laughed out loud. "Ah, Bella," he said, "you never cease to astonish me."

As she had just astonished herself, she was not disposed to demur.

"But why Gisborne for Miss DuChateau? I should think she would much prefer a book on the picturesque, or some such nonsense, to one giving instruction to wives."

Shifting about, she explained, "Well, you said yourself she is of an age to be married. A young lady cannot begin too soon to prepare herself for that event."

"Perhaps she wishes to fall in love first. From what I know of my cousin, she would insist upon a love match. I believe she would require a love match to be happy. I myself have a high regard for love matches. Indeed, I recollect your once saying that you prized a love match above all things."

Isabella was dismayed to hear repeated, not once but several times, the very phrase she had so lately heard from Lady Pillowbank, a phrase which again filled her with a profound sense of what she had let slip away. With an effort, she collected herself, saying, "No doubt your cousin will fall in love before the month is out, six or seven times at least."

"Miss DuChateau is too sensible to be profligate with her affections," he said sternly. "She is not like other females."

Determined to find a point of agreement between them, Isabella said, "Exactly so, and therefore, the gentlemen of the Town are certain to fall in love with her. As she is pretty, modest and silent, the line of her suitors will extend as far as Twickenham."

This observation, far from soothing him, irritated him further. "They may extend as far as Perdition, if they choose, but they will have to get round Wild Goose first."

"A most formidable duenna indeed. Any gentleman who braves that obstacle will deserve to win the hand of the fair Celeste."

"There will be no such gentleman. Wild Goose is ever on the watch."

The fire in his tone induced her to try another tack. "I daresay I need not have alarmed you, for as the good princess knows nothing of the Town, and as Miss DuChateau has no other sponsor, she will be forced to keep indoors. No eligible gentlemen, indeed no human creature whatever, will have the opportunity to set eyes on her, let alone fall in love with her. Miss DuChateau will be quite safe from proposals of marriage and from anything else London affords which might give a young lady ideas of that kind, and so you may rest easy."

She hoped this view of the matter would persuade him that they were not opposed on the subject, but it served only to put him in a brown study. In vain did Isabella attempt to read the meaning behind his sternness. One thing was clear, however: Ashton had had no difficulty in resisting her charms. It seemed he was more likely to conceive a tendre for Lady Pillowbank than for her. It was also clear that he was maddeningly easy in her company, while she was excruciatingly uneasy in his.

They walked to a pond in which a pair of ducks scolded each other. The tassels of the larches hung over the water and showed their reflections in languid shimmers.

Carefully, she said, "Perhaps you will bring Miss DuChateau to call on me. Her brother, too. I will present her with the gift I have bought, and I will endeavour to see what may be done about Mr. DuChateau's dislike."

She steeled herself to hear him decline and was surprised when he did not. Why he should pay polite calls on the woman he intended to cast off was a mystery to her. Nevertheless, she was grateful that he had accepted her invitation.

"And when I bring my cousins to visit," he said amiably, "perhaps Tassie will amuse them while you and I take up a matter of business."

"By business, you mean the divorce." She congratulated herself on having said it without flinching.

"It is odd, I think, that you have not said a word about it. Before I speak to Mr. Doty, I should like to hear what you have to say."

To avoid his scrutiny, she peered into the water as though the lily pad which floated before was a prodigy of nature.

He persisted. "Surely, you have an opinion, however small, on a matter which affects you so nearly."

If only he would not look at her face, she thought, but he did not move his eyes. Forced to say something, she finally hit on a tolerably tranquil reply. "My opinion is this, Tony. It might be well to inform our acquaintance of your intentions. It will not do to have them speak, as Lady Pillowbank did, of your own house and your own bed as though you occupied them."

Harshly, he replied, "When the time comes, the world shall know that we are no longer man and wife, and the announcement will be as vulgar as you could wish. I shall advertise it in the *Times*, if you like. Meanwhile, I should think you would have something more to say than that you wish our private affairs to be made public."

"What more do you wish me to say?" she cried. Then, seeing that her outburst had startled him, she said, lowering her lashes and affecting a tranquil tone, "In a situation such as this, it is the husband's prerogative to do as he wishes. It is the wife's to accede meekly to those wishes."

He laughed. "I know you, Bella. You have never been meek in your life."

She looked up. His smile made her feel suddenly helpless. "You have grown hard, Tony," she murmured. "I remember when Anthony Ashton spoke with gentleness, warmth and candour. You are no longer that man. You may know me, as you claim, but I do not know you."

He raised her hand to his lips, and said with a half smile, "I would not have it any other way."

CHAPTER SEVEN

FOLLOWING THE OUTING in Green Park, Ashton considered well Isabella's observation that Celeste's sojourn in London would be spent in lonely confinement in Upper Berkeley Street. That hint had plunged him into a brown study during their walk and continued to occupy his thoughts for some days afterwards. Because he liked nothing better than finding ways of inspiring his cousin's shy smiles, he wished to find the means of making her stay in London a happy one. He acknowledged that Celeste required a sponsor as well as a protector, someone more suited to dressing her, taking her on morning calls and advising her as to manners and comportment than Wild Goose.

At last he consulted Lady Pillowbank on the matter. Her ladyship asked him why on Earth he wished to put himself to the trouble of employing a virtual stranger when the perfect sponsor resided under his own nose in his own house and was, as his wife, surely ready and eager to look after his young relation. No one was better suited to the task of bringing out a young girl, her ladyship assured him, than his own dear Bella.

Ashton was not disposed to explain why he had not approached Isabella, not only because he had no intention of making the divorce public before he had set it in motion, but also because he thought Lady Pillowbank had hit on an excellent expedient. Bella was well connected, had entrée everywhere, and was too well versed in the follies of the Town to allow Celeste to be taken in by flatterers and flirts. She possessed the gifts of information and understanding and would not fill Celeste's head with nonsense. With her humour, she would laugh Celeste out of any excess of diffidence or terror. She would introduce the girl to impressions which would enlarge her views and refine her taste. In short, he could not agree more with Lady Pillowbank: as a sponsor, Bella would be matchless.

There was one difficulty: the last thing a woman in Bella's situation would wish to do was oblige the husband who meant to cast her off. Any woman would scorn the suggestion. On the other hand, Bella was not any woman. She was unique, and what made her so was her propensity to do a thing simply because she was expected to do the opposite. With that propensity in mind, he determined to make the proposal to her at the earliest opportunity. If she should fling his words angrily in his teeth, he consoled himself, then at least he would have had the pleasure of rousing her ire.

IT SEEMED TO ISABELLA that the walk in Green Park had ended in mutual dissatisfaction. Consequently, she feared that Ashton would not bring his cousins to Hertford Street as promised. Several days of waiting at home in vain bore out her fear, and though ordinarily she liked nothing better than being proved right, in this instance she could not have been more sorry. After enduring as much as she was able of Tassie's fretfulness and her own disquiet, she determined to send the Gisborne volume to Upper Berkeley Street in the hope that this attention to Miss DuChateau would provoke a visit. Before she could summon the messenger to deliver the gift, however, the footman en-

tered the saloon to announce that the very visitors she
desired to see now waited without. She took a moment to caution Tassie to mind what she said and another to summon her courage, then bade the servant
show the visitors in.

Ashton entered with his cousins and Wild Goose.
The young people stopped after a step or two, awed by
the grandeur of the saloon and its furnishings. Celeste exclaimed at the handsomeness of the azure em-
bossed paper, the carved chairs and the row of delicate
figurines on the mantelpiece. Then, evidently conscious that she had been guilty of an excess of fer-
vour, she halted and murmured something unintelligible to the carpet.

Wild Goose took advantage of the silence to admire Isabella's gown of pale yellow muslin and en-
quire whether it might be traded for a hatchet and
twenty gull feathers.

"Will you accept it as a present?" Isabella asked.
"If so, I shall have it sent to you tomorrow."

"I am agreeable," Wild Goose replied, with less
menace than she had heretofore addressed her.

"I think perhaps you are," Isabella replied with a
smile, and seeing that she had contrived to win over
the two ladies, she glanced at Ashton and Guy. There
she found no such complaisance, for the former
seemed preoccupied with putting Celeste at her ease,
while the latter watched Bella through narrowed eyes.

Isabella turned again to Celeste, who gave her such
a pretty, timid smile that she took the girl's hands,
saying, with perfect truth, that she had been most
anxious for such a visit. She then led Celeste to a settee and drew her down beside her. "I am particularly
glad you have come today," she began, "for I was on
the point of sending you this." Here she reached to the

table for the package, which she placed in Celeste's hands. "If I had sent it, I should have deprived myself of the opportunity to give it to you in person. I must know whether you like it."

Overwhelmed, Celeste looked from Ashton, who watched with interest, to Tassie, who crinkled her face, to Guy, who frowned, and finally, to Wild Goose, who had squeezed her bulk into a sofa and now sat like a totem. With each shift, Celeste's eyes welled a little more until they swam.

Isabella, who always delighted in giving presents, only wished she had something of a jollier nature for Celeste. The poor girl must be bored to extinction, she felt, by the dry-as-dust tome she had just received. And it was a great pity, Isabella thought with a sigh, for she was touched by the girl's grateful tears and even more by her gentle manner. When Celeste protested that Mrs. Ashton was too, too generous, Isabella urged her to open the package.

The young lady unwrapped it slowly and painstakingly so as to disturb the string and the paper as little as possible. She then took up the book and gazed reverently at its cumbersome title.

"I hope you will like it," Isabella said. "It is a book on matrimony."

"It does not matter what the subject is. I shall like it because of your kindness in giving it to me. I confess, I did not expect such extraordinary kindness."

"I hope you will find it possible to like it on its own account as well. As Mr. Ashton pointed out to me, you are of marriageable age and it is not too soon to begin to learn all you can. I hope such a book may be welcome."

Celeste glanced at her feet.

Isabella looked at Ashton, who watched attentively, and at Guy, who continued to regard her as sternly as though she were a thief caught with her hand in his pocket. Her heart went out to Celeste, who had only these two gloomy gentlemen and a fearsome Indian to entertain her in London. She wished she could do something for the poor girl. Turning back to Celeste with a sad smile, she said, "You blush very becomingly, but soon, I trust, you will be accustomed to the idea of marrying. It is the duty of all good creatures to marry and bring more of their kind into the world. Heaven knows we have enough of the other sort."

"I have not thought of marriage," Celeste said with a violent blush.

Isabella patted her hand soothingly. "Then you will oblige me greatly if you will put the book away and give it no further thought until you have good reason to think of it." Then, to ward off any further thanks, she suggested a tour of the house.

Tassie agreed to accompany the sister and brother DuChateau and their *yatoro* throughout the rooms. Ashton declined to join them, explaining that business with Isabella claimed him. Even the promise of seeing the new wash-out closet which Isabella had caused to be installed did not induce him to change his mind; he would stay. When the touring party went out in Tassie's wake, Isabella and Ashton were left alone.

ALTHOUGH ASHTON stood at the window with his back to Isabella, he was very much aware of her presence. When he turned to face her, wondering how best to broach the matter which weighed on his mind, she burst out with "Oh, Tony, won't you take pity on poor Miss DuChateau and find the means by which she may be properly introduced to London Society? It is heartless to keep her imprisoned in Upper Berkeley Street with only her brother and Wild Goose to entertain her."

Ashton smiled at the convenient opening. "You are right, it is heartless," he said.

"I am right?" she said, surprised.

He could see that she had anticipated a dispute, and it pleased him to have disappointed her.

Sitting beside her on the sofa, he said, "I have spent the past several days endeavouring to locate a proper sponsor for Celeste, someone who would teach her to appreciate the amusements as well as avoid the pitfalls of polished Society."

"And what is your success?"

"None whatever. Lady Pillowbank, for example, has three daughters to launch. She does not wish to add a rival."

"Lady Pillowbank is wise. If her daughters were to appear in company with Celeste, they would look like two moles and a titmouse, which they in fact are."

"That is not why Lady Pillowbank declined. She naturally wished to know why my wife did not fill the office. It occurred to me that any lady I applied to would ask the same question."

Isabella looked away. "I suppose you told Lady Pillowbank the truth. Well, so be it. What is the use in putting it off?"

"I shall tell the world when I am ready and not before. Besides, Lady Pillowbank is correct."

She regarded him with questioning eyes.

"Why shouldn't Mrs. Ashton sponsor Miss Du-Chateau? There is no one more proper than yourself to do it."

"No one more proper than myself?" she cried. "Proper is the last thing I am."

He laughed. "I did not mean to insult you with such an epithet, but it is manifestly clear that you genuinely like Celeste. I know you well enough to know that you would not hold her beauty against her. Having an ample supply of your own, you would have no need to envy hers."

He saw her press her lips together and suspected that she thought he was deliberately flattering her. In a gentler tone, he added, "Celeste likes you, too, you know. She would not like Lady Pillowbank half so well."

As he waited for her reply, he saw Isabella's expression grow dark. He felt that if ever she was going to hurl recriminations at him and rail like a fishwife, this was the moment.

But she said only, in a subdued voice, "It is very odd that you should choose to have your cousin taken about the Town by the very wife you wish to be rid of."

He nodded, appreciating the irony and the opportunity to share it with one who was equally appreciative. "It is more than odd. It is ridiculous. I quite understand your wishing to decline."

She stood. "I did not say I wished to decline. Did you hear me say anything about declining? I said no such thing. I simply wish you to realize that if I were to agree to such a plan, you and I would be forced to be often in each other's company. I had assumed that that was the very thing you most wished to avoid."

He rose and met her eyes. "Whether I am in your company or out of it, it is all one to me."

If she winced, he could not detect it.

"How clearly and succinctly you express yourself," she responded with a laugh. "I declare, you might stand for the Commons."

"But perhaps such frequent meetings would prove awkward for *you*," he said. "In that case, you would naturally wish to spare yourself the distress. I quite understand."

"Our meetings would not distress me in the least," she retorted. "I am able to tolerate them as well as you."

Seeing the first light of defiance brighten her face, he was amused. "It is true," he said, "that the circumstances in which we find ourselves are generally thought to be conducive to animosity and rancour. Indeed, the world would like nothing so much as the spectacle of our stabbing each other through our respective hearts, but, for my part, I see no reason why we should not be civil. Anything less than civility would be beneath us, in my view."

She straightened her shoulders and lifted her chin. "I value civility quite as much as you do. Indeed, I treasure it above all things."

"Nothing is so charming as civility."

"One may be guilty of many sins, but the worst is incivility."

"We are fortunate to live in an age of civility."

"Yes," she agreed with force, "and we are fortunate to be English, for we scorn to imitate the example of the French and the Americans, who resort to barbarism and savagery when they might just as easily be civil."

"We are fortunate to understand each other so well."

"And you are fortunate, Tony, that I have decided to rescue poor Celeste from the tedium you have supplied her thus far."

"Then you accept?"

"Yes, but I warn you, you had better prepare yourself."

His brows rose and he stepped closer in order to hear the threat.

"We shall spend a great deal of your blunt, Celeste and I. I mean to dress her up and show her off in the best style. I shall expect you to give me carte blanche, so that if you have any hesitation in regard to the expense, you had better say so now, before you find yourself with pockets to let."

"I am not afraid of you," he said, half smiling.

"Oh" was all she said, causing him to wonder if he had disappointed her again.

"I shall inform Celeste of her good fortune."

Isabella said, "I should like to be the one to tell her, or ask her, rather, if I may. She might not like the scheme, you know."

"She will like it. But you may ask her, if it pleases you."

"Then we are agreed."

"Yes."

He put out his hand, and after a moment's hesitation, she extended hers. As they shook hands on the bargain, he noted her eyes were lowered. It seemed to him that she avoided meeting his. That conviction gratified him beyond measure.

When he let go her hand, he congratulated himself on having won his point. Of course, he would need to keep a close watch on Bella. Not that she would lure Celeste into the sort of reckless schemes she favoured for her own amusement, but it was his duty to look after his cousin. Upon reflection, he found he did not object to the obligation. In fact, it suited him very well, for it satisfied his sense of justice to be able to witness the sight of the first Mrs. Ashton grooming the second.

CHAPTER EIGHT

WHEN ASHTON TOOK LEAVE of Isabella and went in search of the others, she wished to go at once to her sitting-room. The nearness of her husband, the agreement they had just made, the sensation of their hands touching and the knowledge that she would now have every opportunity she could wish of renewing his admiration—all had conspired to leave her breathless. She needed a moment alone to consider what this agreement between them meant and why he had sought it. But before she could quit the room, she was interrupted by the sudden appearance of Guy Du-Chateau, looking youthful, handsome and dreadfully cast down.

She could not imagine a less opportune moment for making light conversation or for endeavouring to charm a young man who did not wish to be charmed. However, when he approached and humbly asked if he might sit, she could not very well turn him out of the room. Therefore, she invited him with a gesture to sit beside her on the sofa, and with as much patience as she could summon, said, "You disapprove of my wash-out closet, I collect."

His head snapped up. "What?"

"I cannot think of any reason why you should look as black as you do, unless you do not like the new closet I sent you to see."

Grimly, he said, "I suppose I liked it well enough."

"I am so relieved. I should have been obliged to have it taken out, otherwise."

Oblivious to her irony, he said, "Mrs. Ashton, if I appear somewhat reserved, that is, if my behaviour strikes you as odd, it is because I scarcely know what to say to you."

Seeing her opportunity, she rose and said hastily, "Well, then, I shall leave you to ponder it in solitude. There is nothing like being by oneself for a bit to quiet the nerves and clear the head. It is what I always like to do myself when I am in a muddle."

Standing like a shot, he stopped her. "Please do not go. If I am bumbling, it is because I am not used to doing what I am about to do."

"Good heavens, what are you about to do?"

"Eat crow."

"Sir, I never serve crow to my guests," she said, wondering all the while how she might contrive to leave him. "It is a most noxious dish, and one I have entirely banished from my own regimen. When the tea is served, you shall find nothing but bread and butter and cakes on the table. And now I shall leave you so that you may contemplate the joys in store for you."

"Mrs. Ashton, I beg you to stay. I have seen your conduct towards my sister, I have reviewed all which was spoken between us that night, and I find myself regretting much of what I said. In short, it appears I may have judged you too harshly."

Shaking her head, she said, "You will recall that I advised you to hold off all judgement for two weeks. You must follow that excellent advice, for I am never wrong except on occasion, but as those occasions are scarcely worth mentioning, I shall not mention them. And now, goodbye. I shall rejoin you shortly."

"Stay," he pleaded, and in his eagerness he put his hand on her arm. As his eyes rested on her, she saw that they had lost all their former suspicion. His expression held a hint of warmth which reminded her stingingly of the way Ashton had once looked at her. It jolted her. Quickly, she moved to look out the window.

Guy followed her, attempting to make agreeable conversation. "It will not be long, I suppose, before Tony returns to this house," he said.

When she responded with a look of anguish, he hurried to explain, "I mention it only because I should like to visit again—to inspect your wash-out closet once more and give you a more intelligible opinion than I was able to earlier."

Feeling herself close to tears, she could not look at him. "You need not hold off visiting on Tony's account," she said huskily. "He will remain in St. James's."

"He'll not live in his own house?"

Shaken, she cried, "He intends to seek a divorce!" Instantly she regretted her words. "I ought not to have said that," she murmured, heartsick. "I spoke on impulse. It is a defect I cannot seem to overcome."

He shook his head in disbelief. "Divorce?"

Unable to hide her chagrin, she said, "Please say nothing about it. Tony would not like it."

"You have my promise."

"Say nothing, not even to Celeste."

"If that is what you'd like, I shall keep mum, even to my sister."

"And to me. You must not mention it to me, either. It must be as though I never told you."

"You may trust me not to breathe a word to any soul, living or dead."

Feeling her emotion rise, she put her hand to her lips.

"Would it be impertinent of me to ask what you mean to do—afterwards, I mean?"

Appalled, she stared at him. "Mr. DuChateau, you just gave me your word you would not mention it."

"And I shall keep my word. But I must know what is to become of you."

Unhappily, she said, "I shall travel hither and yon, leading the life of a wanderer. I shall seek refuge abroad with the Princess, where it does not matter if a lady misbehaves, as long as she does it in Italian. Better still, I shall get me to a nunnery, where I may contemplate the error of my ways."

"You make light of it," he said, "but you feel it."

As he stood before her, he gave her an excellent view of a man in the fullness of youth: raw, handsome, eager, reckless. She had liked him from the first because he hated her. She liked him now because he was kind. Indeed, she liked him too well to reprove him very sternly for breaking his vow of silence. "You must not trouble yourself on my account," she said. "I shall do well enough."

With sudden heat, he declared, "I do not give a groat for what anyone says; I mean to visit you—afterwards, I mean." Then, apparently conscious of his impetuosity, he corrected himself. "That is to say, I shall visit you with your permission, of course."

"Only if you keep your word and say no more about it. If you break it again, I shall forbid you to so much as leave your card."

Guy grinned and stated boldly, "That would not stop me."

Bella was spared the necessity of replying to this impertinence by the entrance of the others. She could not tell whether Ashton had been moved by the memories the house evoked, but she was gratified when he complimented her on the acquisition of a new bake-oven.

She contrived to have a private moment with Tassie, enough to tell her of the agreement she had made to sponsor Celeste.

"You did not get him to think better of the divorce?" Tassie asked fretfully.

"Not yet, but I have every hope of doing so, for now I shall not have to invent excuses for meeting him. He has given me precisely what I need."

"Well, do not be too long about it, Bella. You will not mind what I say, of course—you never do—but my nerves cannot withstand the uncertainty forever."

Isabella sent for tea and immediately set about arranging and rearranging everybody comfortably. When the tea things were brought in, the cups filled to steaming and the plates piled with delectables, Isabella surveyed them all and said, "Well, we are very cosy, are we not?"

All eyes fixed on her expectantly. Ashton smiled, knowing from of old that she was about to work her spell.

Isabella continued, "We are so cosy that I should like to make an invitation. It would be my pleasure to introduce Miss DuChateau to my acquaintance, which, as you know, is vast."

Celeste's jaw dropped. Her hands flew to her cheeks and she stammered her gratitude.

"That is singularly generous," Guy said. The news he had lately heard from Isabella had given rise to the natural expectation that she would cut Ashton and his relations and set all her acquaintance against them.

"Not generous at all," Isabella said. "It would re-dound to my credit if I were to make Celeste the rage."

Ashton smiled indulgently at his young cousin, saying, "Well, Celeste, do you wish to be the rage?"

"Oh, I should like it of all things!" she replied.

"Then of course you shall be!" he said warmly.

"I shall never be the rage, for I am ignorant of how to behave in Society. I shall become tongue-tied and disgrace myself, and all of you will be horribly let down."

"Ignorant and tongue-tied young ladies are precisely what London needs," Isabella said. "The Town is full of rattles. Modest silence will be your distinction. All you will have to do is keep mum and listen to everybody's foolishness and they will say that you are wondrously sagacious for so young and pretty a maiden."

"You must heed Bella's advice," Tassie interjected. "She is so well acquainted with the rules of Society that she is able to break them at will."

"Thank you for the encomium, cousin," said Isabella. "You remind me that if I am to teach Celeste how to behave, I shall have to mind my own manners."

Terrified of inconveniencing Isabella, Celeste blurted out, "Oh, do not mind your manners on my account. I should never forgive myself if I were the cause of your behaving properly!"

A pause fluttered in the air like a butterfly. Then everybody burst into gales of laughter. Seeing Celeste flush bright pink, Isabella clasped her hand. "Oh," she said, "I do like you." Celeste turned deep red as Isabella continued, "I shall make all London worship at your feet."

Isabella glanced swiftly at Ashton and found him regarding her with a softer look than she had yet seen. Clearly she had been right, she told herself; the way to his heart was through his cousins. Encouraged, she turned to the ladies and began to talk gaily of muslins and silks. Tassie gave them the benefit of a multitude of opinions, though she was sure no one minded what she had to say, and Wild Goose offered suggestions regarding head-feathers and beads.

Their conversation excluded the gentlemen, who began to speculate on the likelihood of another war between England and the United States. In such an event, what would be the effect felt in Canada? Guy asked. It went without saying, Ashton replied, that in such a case, they would return at once to do whatever needed to be done.

Turning the topic, Guy asked, "Tony, do you approve of our all being 'cosy,' as Mrs. Ashton suggests? I should think you would object."

"Why should I object?"

Recalling his promise to Isabella not to breathe a word with regard to the divorce, Guy bit back the response on his tongue and did not pursue the subject. Instead he observed, "I suppose you think my sister must benefit from an intimacy with the granddaughter of a duke."

"Yes, she will. Celeste began by being terrified of Bella. Then she pitied her. Now she is on the point of worshipping her. This enterprise will give her the opportunity to find a middle ground. More important, Isabella will teach Celeste to see beneath the surfaces. With Bella to tutor her, she is not likely to be taken in by flatterers and knaves."

"I envy Celeste."

"Would you, too, like to be the rage?" Ashton asked. "If so, I shall put a word in Bella's ear."

"I thank you for the favour, but if I should desire it, I prefer to put the word in her ear myself."

"Then you do not absolutely object to meeting her?" Ashton said in a more serious tone. "I am glad, for I know how you dislike her. I would not wish this proposed intimacy to tax your patience unduly."

Guy shrugged off any suggestion that he would be made uncomfortable by an intimacy with Isabella Ashton. "Oh, I shall do well enough," he said cheerfully. "In fact, I look forward to improving my acquaintance with her. I have never seen anything quite like Mrs. Ashton's sangfroid. She is remarkable."

Ashton was glad to observe the thaw in the young man and concluded that Isabella, in the space of half an hour, had captivated his cousins. More than her charm, he guessed, they admired her good nature. And, he acknowledged, it *was* admirable. Her absence of rancour was extraordinary, so extraordinary, in fact, that he could not but wonder what the deuce she was plotting. Unpredictable and contrary though she was, he could not quite believe that she would foster a cosiness which must be painfully awkward unless she hoped somehow to gain by it.

In the hope of finding out more, he drew Bella apart from the others as they took their leave. Their conversation was pleasant enough, but yielded no clue. At last he hit on the expedient of taking her into his confidence. Perhaps, he thought, she might be induced to do the same.

Accordingly, he said, "Bella, I have a confession to make."

The effect of these words pleased him. She grew white.

"I watched you when you had no notion I was anywhere near. In short, I spied on you."

Puzzled, she gazed into his eyes.

"I followed you into Hatchard's some days ago. I overlistened your conversation."

He observed Isabella frantically trying to recall what she had said to Lady Pillowbank on that occasion, and with noble forbearance, he did not betray even the hint of a smile.

"If I spoke in my usual fashion," she said uneasily, "I no doubt said something I ought not to have said."

"I do not like having played the spy, Bella. It's the sort of thing one hoots at in French plays. My defence is that I did intend to make myself known to you, but Lady Pillowbank kept to your side the entire time."

"It is no use trying to recollect my words," she said in an anxious tone. "I cannot remember them. I hope you will forget anything I may have said that was not quite the thing."

"If you can forget what I did, I can forget what you said."

A bargain was struck between them, and once again they shook hands, but he felt no closer to knowing her intentions. Whatever scheme was afoot, he thought as he parted from her, he would have to unearth it in the days and weeks ahead. Meanwhile, it would gratify him to know that Bella would plague herself for days trying to recall what he had heard her say in the bookstore.

ISABELLA SCARCELY GAVE the bookshop a thought, however. What struck her as astonishing in Ashton's revelation was that he had taken the trouble to follow her into Hatchard's and listen to her conversation.

This was conduct so singular, so unforeseen, that it gave her the first real glimmer of hope she had known since he had spoken the word *divorce*. She had feared that he was too angry with her ever to be won over, but now her fear turned to elation. The act he had just confessed to meant that she continued to exert some influence upon him, however small, that he felt an irresistible pull towards her, and though it might not yet be as great as the pull he had once felt or the pull she felt towards him, it was something, at least. She was almost sure of it now: in spite of himself, a part of him loved her still.

CHAPTER NINE

ONLY ONCE had Ashton had the opportunity to see Celeste in raptures. On that occasion, when he had consented to allow her and her brother to accompany him to England, she had shed tears of happiness and sworn that no creature had ever been blessed with such an amiable cousin. The second occasion occurred directly after their visit to Isabella, when he found himself alone with Celeste in the sitting-room in Upper Berkeley Street. Barely containing her joy, Celeste knelt at his feet as he sat in a great chair, then suddenly seized his hand and murmured a torrent of thanks.

Smiling, he took in the sight of her lovely face. Her simplicity, earnestness and grace charmed him utterly. In Bella's presence, he felt the air so thick with electricity that he must ever be on guard. Celeste's companionship, by contrast, never failed to soothe.

"You need not thank me," he said. "Bella wished to do something for you. She likes nothing better than dressing up and going about the Town, and when she tires of dressing herself, she likes nothing better than to dress a young lady who will do her credit."

"I shall always be grateful to Mrs. Ashton. She is generosity itself. But you need not disparage your part in the plan. You must permit me to thank you, too."

He placed his hand over hers. "Please do not. It gives me pleasure to see you happy. That is all the thanks I require."

Playfully, she shook her fair curls. "I will not be prevented from thanking you, despite what you say. I am well aware that I owe you all my present good fortune and I *will* thank you for it. I shall not be stopped."

Laughing into her large brown eyes, he said, "I never met a less stubborn female in my life."

She blushed furiously, saying, "It is true that as a rule I prefer to set aside my own wishes and give others their way, but in this instance, I intend to stand my ground. What do you say to that?" She looked at him with an uncharacteristic gleam of determination in her eyes.

This show of strength in the girl moved Ashton. He had long hoped to see her exhibit a little fire. Much as he prized her docility, he cared too much for her to see her be a mere cipher. Indeed, one of the reasons he had wished Bella to sponsor her was that she would bring to the forefront any spark the girl possessed. At this moment, as he studied her shining face, he would have liked to kiss her. It would have pleased him even more to be able to respond to her challenge with a proposal of marriage. Because honour imposed silence on him, however, he answered with only a cousinly, "Well, then, thank me if you must. I cannot deny you anything." Soon after, he took leave of her, thinking how glad he was that he was engaged to wait on Mr. Doty in his chambers the very next day.

MR. DOTY, who had been happily married to four wives in the space of thirty-eight years, was shocked and saddened to learn that a man as fine, rich and genteel as Mr. Ashton contemplated divorce. He himself had been parted from his wives by the expediency of death and believed that that method was greatly to be preferred over so costly and unsavoury a proceeding as divorce. Thus it was that the lawyer did what he could to dissuade Ashton from such an extreme measure.

"You may eventually squeeze a private bill of divorce out of Parliament," Mr. Doty explained, "but it will be dreadfully expensive."

"I am prepared to bear the expense, whatever it may be."

"Dear me. This does not bode well," Mr. Doty replied. "When courting a lady, one's spending is obliged to be lavish. But when it is a matter of parting, one ought not to run up bills. I know whereof I speak, if I may say so. Have I not myself been blessed with four wives?"

"I have all that is necessary and more to cover the expense. If it would hasten the business, I would willingly pay twice the sum."

"What you do not realize, sir, is that divorce is a lengthy, arduous affair. First, you must obtain a decree of judicial separation in the Ecclesiastical Courts. Then you must petition for a private bill in Parliament specifically dissolving your marriage. In support of your petition, you must win a verdict of damages in the Common Law Courts against your wife's seducer. Divorce is such a vast deal of vexation and bother that it is no wonder only two or three are granted in a year."

"It shall be your purpose to see that I am one of the fortunate few, and I would be obliged if you would see to it immediately."

"Could you not reconcile your differences with Mrs. Ashton? I should be happy to do what I may as intermediary, if you like."

"I thank you, but no, Mr. Doty. You see, I wish to remarry."

"Well! That is a desire with which I can fully sympathize, if I may say so, as I have been seized with a similar desire twenty times at least in my lifetime and have acted upon it in several momentous instances. But," he added in a cautionary tone, "as divorce is so very difficult, you may wish to consider an alternative."

"I have never heard that there was a lawful alternative."

"Oh, yes indeed! As I mentioned earlier, in order to divorce, you are required to obtain a decree of judicial separation from the Ecclesiastical Courts. This separation is, in itself, a form of divorce, that is to say, a divorce from bed and board. *A mensa et thoro,* it is called. It is distinguished from divorce *a vinculo matrimonii,* meaning 'the chains of matrimony,' which only Parliament can grant. The *a mensa et thoro* decree can allow you to separate from your wife without the expense of a bill in Parliament or a verdict in the Common Law Courts. In this manner you may save yourself a prodigious deal of time and expense."

"It does seem an unnecessarily complicated business."

"Unnecessarily! No indeed, sir. If it were less complicated, half the husbands in Britain would divorce, the middle classes would divorce, perfect nobodies would divorce. Wives might even take it into their heads to divorce their husbands, for the law in its infinite wisdom has not seen fit to prevent such an eventuality.''

"But what of the alternative, Mr. Doty? You said there was an alternative.''

"Yes, indeed. You may content yourself with *a mensa et thoro* and go no further. Then, you may live with the lady who has taken your fancy as though she were your wife. Any children resulting from such an arrangement might be well provided for. I have drawn up the papers in numerous such cases. The matter of matrimony need never be raised at all. Such a separation is frequently done and perfectly lawful.''

Ashton replied severely, "I do not like your alternative, Mr. Doty. I will not live with the lady without benefit of marriage. I would not place her in such a position. Her honour is as much to me as my own.''

"Honour! Nothing can be accomplished where there is an insistence upon honour.''

"But I do insist upon it, Mr. Doty.''

The lawyer would have expatiated further, but Ashton silenced him with a raised hand. "Good day,'' he said. "I leave you to get on with the matter as speedily as possible.''

"But I have not told you all, sir.''

"You have told me enough, more than enough. I will hear the rest another time. I am engaged to Mrs. Ashton and am already late.''

Mr. Doty's eyes widened. "Engaged to Mrs. Ashton? I thought it was many years since your mother had passed from this vale of tears.''

"I am speaking of my wife, who is still very much alive. She wishes me to attend her and my cousins to Mr. Wedgwood's warehouse.'' He took up his hat and moved to the door.

Mr. Doty cried, "I do not understand, sir. You cannot mean to visit the shops in the company of the selfsame woman you intend to divorce."

Ashton enquired, "Must I first obtain a decree or a bill or a verdict before my wife and I may be allowed to purchase a bit of crockery?"

"It is unheard of. I should think you would not wish to speak to her, let alone travel about the Town in her company. I should think, if you are so determined to divorce her, that you are angry with her, and she with you."

"That is not the case," Ashton replied, unable to resist a gleam of irony. "We are not angry. Indeed—" and here he smiled "—you will be happy to know that Mrs. Ashton and I are perfectly cosy."

NOTHING SPURRED Isabella's genius like a campaign. In this respect, she resembled Wellington, with whom she felt a kinship, for both were required to organize their strategy, marshal their forces and capture enemy territory. But while Wellington was obliged to wage his campaign on foreign soil, Isabella had the advantage of knowing every inch of her battleground. Had the war been fought in Canada, she would have given little for her chances. As it was, London had to be the scene of triumph.

She divided her campaign into three principal operations: shopping, visiting and touring. Celeste must be made familiar with Bond Street; she must positively burn her unfashionable clothes and purchase new ball dresses, bonnets and baubles, without which her march upon the Town could scarcely succeed. Furthermore, the girl must be made welcome at the houses of the Town's most influential wives and mothers, those ladies who possessed the power to make her an icon or an outcast simply by the wave of a fan or the crook of a finger. Finally, Celeste had to see London, its parks, palaces and pleasures, and learn to behold them without falling into ecstasies.

The initial volley in the shopping operation was fired during the visit to Mr. Wedgwood's warehouse, where, after several hours of timid study, Celeste was induced to purchase a jasperware teapot for her mama. Isabella found, to her amazement, that Celeste was terrified of running up bills. Despite the respectable income of the DuChateau family and Ashton's generosity, the child suffered from a streak of frugality which paralyzed her in the face of beautiful, expensive objects available for sale. Regardless of what Isabella said to reassure her, Celeste was incapable of selecting so much as a saucer without a tremble of the lips and a catch in the voice.

Isabella had heard of creatures who did not like to spend money, but she had never met one in the flesh. At last, in exasperation, she said, "I wish you would realize, Miss DuChateau, that by spending his money, you would make your cousin the happiest man alive. Am I not right, Tony?"

They had stopped in a stationer's, where Celeste had struggled for upwards of half an hour to purchase a bit of writing paper.

Ashton laughed. "You are indeed right, Bella. I should like Celeste to please herself, and not just with a pretty paper, but with a new parasol or a pretty brooch."

"It would make you happy?" Celeste exclaimed, incredulous. She appeared to believe that if one had money, one could do only one thing: lay it up. The notion that spending it could bring pleasure was entirely new.

"Of all things, it will make him happiest," Isabella said, not scrupling to exaggerate. "I recollect that he was never so delighted as when he settled all my bills at the end of a year. Weren't you, Tony?"

She threw Ashton a mischievous look, which he returned in equal measure.

Lovely and charming as she was, Celeste was nearly devoid of humour, or, at any rate, of that sense of irony in which Isabella excelled. Therefore, she took Isabella exactly at her word. If it would make her cousin happy, she would spend his money. She proceeded to do so, thenceforth, with a vengeance, so that it now became Isabella's part to restrain Celeste from acquiring more silk stockings, shawls, shifts and shoes than could be worn by any three young ladies in a lifetime. More than once Isabella felt obliged to apologize to Ashton for having transformed Celeste so monstrously, but as he smiled indulgently and appeared content, she grew easy again.

In all other respects, Celeste proved a worthy protégée. Dressmakers and milliners cooed over her as they discovered that her figure was quite perfect for showing off their gowns and bonnets. They lauded her patience, observing that there were few girls her age who could endure being pinned and fitted for hours on end while her relations went off to the picture gallery or the park. Once she was attired in the latest fashion, Celeste attracted admiring glances everywhere she went. Most important, Ashton was pleased. In Isabella's hearing, he often whispered to Celeste that she was in great beauty.

The girl seemed so young, so guileless, so inexperienced in the ways of the world that Isabella's heart went out to her and she determined to transmit to Celeste some of her great store of wisdom. She wished to

instil in her a less retiring, less docile, more confident
mode of behaviour. It would do no good to teach the
girl to distinguish those who merely flattered from
those who might be trusted if she did not have the
spirit to dismiss the former and encourage the latter.

Isabella felt that at Celeste's age she herself would
have profited mightily from the advice and care of an
older woman. Because her mother had died when she
was a child, she had been left to her own devices and
had taken as her models a rebellious father and an
autocratic grandfather. Emulating them had given her
a reputation for directness and fearlessness, a reputation which now struck her as wholly undeserved, for
whenever she encountered a difficulty with Ashton,
she was, she felt, the soul of indirection and fearful-
ness. Too afraid to speak her heart, she looked to attain her ends by stratagem. That tactic had undone her
once before; in the end, her husband had gone away,
and not merely to the country, or to Scotland or Ireland, where discontented husbands generally went, but
to Canada, halfway round the world. For two years,
she had lived with the knowledge that Ashton had felt
compelled to put an entire ocean between them. And
now that he had returned, she was no more able to
speak openly to him than before.

But *her* fate would not also be Celeste's, she vowed.
She liked the girl too well to see her miserable. She
believed she could assist Celeste in overcoming her
diffidence, and meant to do all in her power to see her
happy.

Because Isabella was little given to self-deception,
she never once said to herself that the present campaign had been undertaken for Celeste's sake. The
principal beneficiary was to be herself. She loved her
husband more than she had loved him as a young

bride. She loved his ironic smile, his steadiness, his solidity of character and, now that she had reason to think he loved her a little, too, she wanted only to spend the rest of her life making up to him the time they had lost.

THE VISITING OPERATION was inaugurated with a march on Lady Sefton's house. Isabella's plan was to begin with skirmishes; not until her troops had been thoroughly seasoned would she attack the best-defended fortresses. Because Lady Sefton was ever known for her liberality of mind, her cordiality and her kind heart, Isabella knocked at her door first.

Lady Sefton, who liked Isabella and valued the relief she afforded from the sameness of London Society, graciously welcomed the brother and sister from Canada. Within two minutes of meeting them, she liked them. It was clear that the young gentleman would cut a fine figure in any drawing-room, while the young lady was as prettily behaved as any young lady just out of the schoolroom ought to be. As a sign of her approval, she promised them vouchers for Almack's and treated them to a drink of her favourite green tea mixture.

Once Lady Sefton had been won, other skirmishes were fought, and as far as Bella was concerned, they were victorious, for she was continually thrown together with Ashton and in a manner which could not fail to advance her cause. At one card party, she happened to be placed opposite him as his partner. With each discard, each draw, their eyes met. They were required to read each other's expressions over the clubs and hearts and to guess what trump cards the other held.

At another card party, they were placed at different
tables, but so near each other that their elbows
knocked more than once. Each knock produced apol-
ogies, smiles and pleasantries, and though a knock on
the elbow might be thought to be more of a nuisance
than an emblem of love, especially during a lively
game of speculation, still each touch sent a shiver of
excitement through her.

One evening, Ashton brought his cousins to Hertford Street, and as the rain threatened to do violence
to Celeste's new-curled hair, and as Isabella was willing to provide a supper of cold pigeon and pudding,
they decided not to go out but instead to play at
acrostics, anagrams and charades. While the puzzles
terrified Celeste, confounded Tassie and mystified
Guy, Ashton and Bella delighted in them. They
guessed each other's riddles before the others even had
a chance to think. When the others accused them of
cheating, Ashton replied with a laugh, "We do not
need to stoop so low."

"You ought not to be allowed to play," Guy said.
"You know each other far too well," a remark which
could not fail to buoy Bella's hopes.

"It is not that we know each other so well," Ashton said. "It is only that we are adept at games, are we
not, Bella?"

The smile he directed at her on this sally sent her
spirits soaring. His teasing seemed to confirm that in
spite of what had passed between them, they remained kindred spirits. That kinship must eventually
succeed, she told herself, in resurrecting what he had
once felt.

Isabella's hopes continued sunny until she found
herself alone with Ashton during one of the visits to
Hertford Street. These visits had become so frequent

that she had begun to think of them as family parties. While Bella seated herself before the pianoforte, Ashton leant upon it easily and informed her that he had seen Mr. Doty.

Bella froze. "You saw Mr. Doty?" It struck her suddenly that she had permitted her imagination to deceive her. She had fancied that Ashton had forgotten his promised visit to the lawyer, that, indeed, he had forgotten the motive for the visit. Obviously, she scolded herself, her wishes had got the better of her sense.

"I delayed mentioning the visit, as I knew it would vex you," he said.

"It does not vex me in the least to hear you speak of Mr. Doty," she protested. "If I seemed a trifle tongue-tied, it is because I had completely forgotten about him."

"You forgot?" he said, with an edge to the words. "Apparently my mentioning that I intended to make such a visit made little impression on you."

His sharpness mortified her, so that she hurried to explain, "I suppose in all the pleasure of dressing Celeste and taking her about I neglected to think of anything disagreeable."

He glanced at her. "I see. You do not find the notion of my visiting Mr. Doty worth remembering, but you do find it disagreeable."

Heat flushed her cheeks. "I never like to remember what is disagreeable. Do you?" Then, to turn him from the subject, she waved a hand in the direction of his young cousin and said, "You must go and ask Celeste to show you her skill at dancing the quadrille. She has been practicing hours and hours, marching up and down the saloon with the dancing master until she has quite worn the polish from the floor. She is wonder-

fully proud of herself and you must commend her
ability to count the steps without moving her lips."

He smiled a little, saying, "If I distressed you by
mentioning Mr. Doty, I beg your pardon."

She looked down. "Please do not disappoint Celeste."

"I do not require persuasions to ask my cousin to
dance," he said. "It will be my pleasure."

When at last Isabella could raise her eyes, she saw
him walking through the intricacies of squares and
turns with Celeste, while Tassie and Guy trilled a tune
for them. She turned away so that she would not be
obliged to watch the cheerful scene.

Privately she acknowledged that she had made little progress. She had thought that by capturing several prestigious citadels she had won the war. On the
contrary, she saw, she had vastly overestimated the
power of her weaponry. It was time to reconnoitre and
shore up her arsenal. She must not march again until
she was more certain of her army, for if Ashton did
indeed love her, it was obvious he did not yet know it.

CHAPTER TEN

ISABELLA WROTE to her grandfather, hinting that she wished him to use his influence to procure an invitation to a fête at Carlton House to be given on the nineteenth of June. Reports of the grand entertainment were rife throughout the Town, including the rumour that the gentlemen would wear either court or military dress. All of London sought to attain a place on the list of the invited, of which there were to be fully two thousand. In that vast number, she wrote to the Old Duke, surely two charming, attractive young Canadians might be included. Her hope was to prove to Ashton that she was so anxious to help his cousins as to put her grandfather's influence at their disposal. Perhaps when he saw to what lengths she was willing to go, he might soften towards her.

Instead of bringing the desired invitation, her note brought the duke himself to Hertford Street. He arrived red-faced, a colouring not produced by rouge and not palliated by the inflammation in his toe.

Isabella was out, having gone with Ashton and his cousins to see a review in the Pall Mall. In her absence, Tassie received the Old Duke in the saloon. She enquired after his health and apologized frequently for inflicting her presence on his sight. The Old Duke, who never minded what Tassie said, sank into a chair and waved Isabella's note under her nose.

"What can she mean by such a request?" he demanded. "Does she think the Prince invites nobodies to Carlton House? And why does she curry favour with Ashton and his upstart relations? She ought to have nothing to do with them."

Nervously, Tassie babbled the explanation, to wit, that Isabella was obliged to curry favour, else Mr. Ashton would divorce her.

"Divorce!"

"That is his intention, I fear."

"Is the fellow lost to all sense of what is due the noblest family in the kingdom, excepting the Hanovers, of course? Divorce should never be permitted, under any circumstances. Marriage is bad enough without divorce entering into it, too."

Unhappily, Tassie said, "Bella says he has visited his solicitor on the matter. Tony appears convinced that they must part forever."

He waved his hand as though a gnat had buzzed his nose. "What is that to say to anything? What husband does not wish to part from his wife? Do you think I did not wish to rid myself of the duchess, who drove me distracted with her relentless good cheer? Morning, teatime, night, she was always singing and saying bright things. It was insupportable, but I did not divorce her. I should never have brought such a scandal upon the family."

"And neither will Bella. She means to prevent the divorce."

He fixed her with his glass. "I do not see how she proposes to prevent it with an invitation to a fête at Carlton House. If there is any logic in that, I should like to know what it is."

Tassie screwed up her courage to answer, "She means be on good terms with Tony, and to that end she is generous to his cousins."

The Old Duke scowled. "You are certain she intends to remain married to this fellow?"

"Oh, yes, do please be reassured on that head, your grace."

On this, the duke looked dismal. His disliked Anthony Ashton through and through. He would never reconcile himself to an alliance with the descendant of a candlemaker. Worse, Anthony Ashton had never confessed his own lowliness. He was a conceited puppy who seemed not to know that his connection to the Wortwells was an honour which he scarcely deserved. The duke was obliged to disapprove of the divorce, but he was not obliged to approve of the marriage.

On that sour thought, he drank a glass of brandy, swore at his toe and took himself off, warning that if he did go to the trouble of procuring the invitation to the fête, all but Isabella would have to content themselves with dining in a tent in the garden, and they must not flatter themselves with the hope of actually setting eyes on the Regent.

ON ASHTON'S NEXT VISIT to Mr. Doty, he had the satisfaction of learning that the necessary applications had been made in the Ecclesiastical Courts. He might expect no difficulty, his lawyer informed him, in receiving a decree of judicial separation. But he must be patient; such things took time.

"You have done well," Ashton said. "I trust you will lose no time in initiating whatever else is required."

"As you wish, sir, but I beg you will permit me first to suggest an alternative."

"If it is no better than your last alternative, Mr. Doty, you may as well save your breath to cool your porridge."

"I feel it my duty to mention, sir, before I proceed any further, that it may be possible, though it is highly unlikely, to have your marriage to Mrs. Ashton declared invalid. That is to say, you may be entitled to an annulment. As I say, such a thing is rare, but in your case, there might be a way."

"Go on, Mr. Doty, but briefly, if you would."

"If I am not mistaken, there has been no issue resulting from your marriage. When a couple is married some years and no children are produced, certain deductions may be made, deductions which, if they be not contradicted, may entitle you to say that you were never in fact married, except in name."

Anthony Ashton was a man who always sat tall and straight in a chair and, in general, appeared sardonic. He now sat even taller and straighter, and looked so forbidding that a clerk who tiptoed into the chamber at that moment was inspired to flee again. For a considerable time, Ashton sat in silence. Nothing was heard in the chamber but the ticking of the clock and the rumblings of hunger in Mr. Doty's stomach.

Slowly, by degrees, and with visible effort, Ashton regained his composure. His grip on the chair was loosened and his expression relaxed somewhat. When he was certain that he had collected himself, he said in a voice which betrayed no emotion, "I shall not need to trouble you with an annulment, Mr. Doty. There *was* a child of my marriage. The boy died before he was a year old."

ASHTON ESCORTED CELESTE to Drury Lane, and while she wept over the tragedy of young Romeo and Ju-

liet, he thought of William. The child's bright blue
eyes and rosy cheeks had filled his imagination from
the moment of leaving Mr. Doty's chambers. He recalled the baby's wet laughter, which had moved him
with its poignancy. He recalled the way in which the
boy had reached out his plump little hands and cried
for his mama. He recalled Isabella resting her cheek
against his fair head and closing her eyes as though
endeavouring to preserve the softness of the moment.
Though it had been more than two years since he had
permitted himself to remember, since his conversation with Mr. Doty, he had been unable to forget.

The time of the boy's illness and death were a haze
to him, much like the mists of Avalon, a haze of dull
pain. Only the vaguest memories remained of what he
had said or how he had conducted himself. As for
Isabella, he had for so long refused to remember her
words and conduct that he could not now remember
them at all. It was as though he had not been there
during that time, as if the best part of himself had
been carried off and the rest had gone in search of it.
He had remained in this state until Bella had informed him that she loved Philip Mattingly and meant
to live with him as his wife. That announcement had
succeeded in jolting him out of his numbness, but it
had turned his grief to gall. Bitterness had overpow-
ered every other feeling. He could not so much as look
at Bella, let alone speak to her, and to get as far from
her as possible, he had set sail for the New World.

"Oh, it is the most enchanting thing!" Celeste exclaimed, bringing him abruptly back to the present.

He knew that she had never seen an actor of the
calibre of Edmund Kean. If the man was too old for
the part and played it as though he considered it an
onerous duty, she was too innocent and kind to see it.

The actor's voice, passion and physical presence had
swept her entirely into the story. Now, as the curtain
fell, she turned to him, her eyes alight with tears of
pleasure, and he knew that the moment she looked
into his eyes, she would guess that something troubled him. To spare her the concern she would suffer,
he looked away. Immediately, he spied Guy in a
nearby box with Isabella.

Ashton excused himself, leaving Celeste with a bevy
of admirers and a stalwart Wild Goose to keep them
at bay. In another minute, he entered Isabella's box.

He stopped in the entry, the curtain in his hand,
looking at Isabella in a new way: as the woman with
whom he shared a sorrow. They had never acknowledged it, never even spoken the boy's name since his
death, but the bond existed between them. Even after
he divorced Bella, he knew, William's memory would
continue to connect them. He wondered if she, too,
felt the connection.

It was impossible for him to pursue that line of
thought, for Guy turned at that moment and saw him.
Engaged in chatting with Isabella, he had been alive
with energy. As soon as his eyes fell on Ashton, however, he grew sullen and irritable. Ashton had the distinct impression that his cousin wished him elsewhere,
on the other side of the world, in fact, for the young
man neither welcomed him nor invited him to sit. It
was left to Bella to say what was proper.

When she did, he sat very near her, and as he saw
Guy's face grow dark, it struck him that the young
man had undergone a singular change. He no longer
resented Isabella. Indeed, he seemed to admire her as
profoundly now as he had scorned her in the past. The
young Canadian was regarding Isabella much as the

lovesick Romeo stared at his little Juliet. Ashton suspected he might be in a fair way to falling in love.

Because he was engrossed in these observations, Ashton scarcely noticed that Isabella was gazing at him in the strangest manner. When at last he did notice, he found that he could scarcely speak. Though ordinarily a man of unfailing politeness, he found it impossible to pretend that he wished to talk of inconsequential matters. At this moment, he could only think of their son. Stiffly, he offered a hasty farewell and went from the box, and though he knew Isabella and Guy would think it odd that he had had nothing to say for himself, he could not do otherwise. After taking a moment to collect himself, he rejoined Celeste and Wild Goose, and endured the rest of the play without hearing a word of it.

Isabella did not hear a word, either. Ordinarily, she would have thrilled to hear Romeo woo Juliet beneath her balcony. Now his words grated like the screeching of blackbirds. Ordinarily, she would have wept at the misunderstandings which caused the two young lovers to die at their own hands in a cold, white crypt. Now she thought the Bard a heartless creature who had deliberately thwarted a perfectly charming married couple when he might just as easily have permitted them to live out the rest of their lives in peace and harmony. Ordinarily, *Romeo and Juliet* was her favourite play; now, she could scarcely contain her impatience for the final couplet.

Disquiet had overtaken her the instant Ashton had appeared in the box. His expression was so serious, so grieved, that she knew he was suffering some anguish. That knowledge oppressed, for the incongruity of her situation had never been more apparent: she was his wife, but she could not extend her hand to him and ask him what was the matter. She was his wife, but she could not comfort him. She was his wife, but was restrained from being wifely. The tragedy on the stage was nothing to the emptiness she felt.

In her preoccupation with Ashton, she failed to give her escort the attention he sought. Guy took her to task for insensibility to the great Kean's performance, and she submitted to be scolded, too distressed by what she had seen in Ashton's face to defend herself. When Guy left her in Hertford Street, she sat for some hours in her sitting-room to think what she might do, and at last concluded that if she could not console her husband, she might at least make him smile. To that end, she resolved to send him an invitation that very night. He must bring Celeste and Wild Goose to her on Tuesday, she wrote. He must not fail her on any account. And he must be prepared to be vastly surprised!

THE SURPRISE was Mrs. Nitney, a silhouette artist who had apprenticed with Mrs. Harrington of Bath and had come to Hertford Street at Isabella's request to trace everybody's profile. She would then cut out the silhouette and present the original with a likeness suitable for hanging.

Wild Goose had sent her regrets—she was engaged to bring a cake of tobacco to the Old Duke, but the rest of the company gathered in the blue saloon, where they were all instructed to be cosy. Celeste was asked to be the first to sit. As Mrs. Nitney worked her deft fingers, she glanced from her lovely model to her paper and back again.

While Mrs. Nitney was thus engaged, Ashton observed Celeste. Dressed in a white muslin selected by Isabella, with her hair in a new style rimmed with curls, she looked exquisite. If they were ever so fortunate as to have children, he mused, he trusted they would favour their mother. That hope consoled him whenever his thoughts turned to William.

Guy sat near his sister, endeavouring to spoil her pose by provoking her to laugh. Isabella sat on Mrs. Nitney's right hand, providing Guy with a view of her profile. It appeared to Ashton that he availed himself of this view rather often. As the young man looked at Bella, his eyes glowed. His behaviour confirmed the suspicion Ashton had formed at Drury Lane: Guy was falling in love.

What Isabella's feelings were, Ashton could not tell. She was certainly conscious that the young man caressed her with his eyes. There were times when she seemed to flush, especially when she caught him looking, but whether the colour was brought on by anger, consciousness or affection, he could not say.

Guy's looks contained such fullness, such fire, that Ashton was reminded of himself at that age. He recollected the urgency which had filled him the moment he had first glimpsed Isabella. The reminder made him restless.

He wished to speak to Guy, to warn him outright, but he thought better of it. What if Guy were too far in over his head to heed a friendly warning? These ardent fellows never listened to reason. They always carried things their own way. Indeed, giving them warnings only fixed their minds more firmly on their object. Had he not done the same? Had he not deprecated his father's warnings that he would be sorry if he married a Wortwell, a line noted for headstrong behaviour? Had he not delighted in defying such warnings? Had he not been too much in love to listen to reason? He did not expect Guy to behave with any more wisdom than he had done.

It was futile, he concluded, to speak to Guy. But he would speak to Isabella. There he had some influence, he knew. Her future condition depended on him. Her ability to maintain a carriage, an establishment in England and a suitable style of living depended on his future provision. He would not stoop to threatening her with penury if she did not obey his wishes, but her consciousness of his power must prompt her to behave with greater circumspection towards Guy.

Therefore, at the first opportunity, he said, "Would it be possible for us to be private, Bella? I would have a word with you."

The request gave her a tightness in the throat. She could not tell whether she most desired or dreaded such an interview. Despite the fact that she had arranged the evening for this very purpose, despite the fact that she longed to have a minute alone with him so as to learn what troubled him, now that it had been accomplished, she was a little frightened.

They stepped into a chamber that he remembered well. It had been a study to which he had repaired for the purpose of reading, thinking, and, in the last months of their life together, brooding. Not a stick of furniture, not a book, not an ornament had been moved. The only difference appeared to be the presence of a handkerchief next to the lexicon, a novel on the great chair, a shawl by the fireplace—all belonging to Isabella.

She did not know whether they were to sit or to stand. Although she was famous for her insouciance, she experienced an excruciating lack of polish. If there was something cordial or light-hearted she was supposed to say now, she could not think what it might be.

At last they sat, he on a high-backed chair near the empty grate, she on a delicate, scarlet-cushioned chair opposite.

"Bella," he began, and as always, the intimate form of address quickened her breathing, "are you aware that Guy DuChateau admires you?"

"Yes, I believe he imagines he admires me. It is quite adorable of him, I think."

"You speak as though he were a child."

"That is what he is."

"He is a man—a young man, to be sure—but a man for all that."

Isabella had not expected the interview to dwell on Guy DuChateau. She had hoped Ashton would be brought to confide to her the cause of his troubled air. Disappointed, she answered, "There is no real attachment, I am convinced. How could there be? He must fall in love with someone younger, not older, than himself, a girl who will think that every word which falls from his lips a perfect pearl and every lock of his hair a veritable sunbeam." This pronouncement, she thought, must settle the matter, permitting her to turn the conversation, but to her dismay, it did no such thing.

"You are his senior by three or four years. That is nothing, at least not when you are in the fullest bloom of womanhood and he is full of admiration."

So that was how he saw her: in the fullest bloom of womanhood! All the flaws of face and figure of which she was so conscious apparently escaped him. She sent up a small prayer of thanks. More tranquil now, she smiled, assuring him, "Yes, he is full of admiration—for any new female acquaintance who crosses his path, and for that reason, he will soon lose interest in me. Another week or two in Society and some young damsel will cause him to forget me entirely. Now, what is it that you wished to speak with me about?''

"He is in love with you, Bella. You would do well to have a care for his heart.''

A new idea seized her. This talk of Guy DuChateau might be very much to the point, after all. It was possible that Ashton had brought her to the study specifically to discuss Guy. It was possible, just possible, that he was jealous. Jealousy might have been the reason for his preoccupation at the theatre. He had seen her with Guy, observed the young man's gallantry and assumed the worst.

Taking a breath, she forced herself to stop thinking such thoughts. She did not wish to form premature conclusions as she had done earlier. Once again she might be allowing her wishes to get the better of her sense. Yet what else was she to think?

And what was she to do? She certainly did not wish to assuage his jealousy, if he were jealous. Prudence dictated that she let him squirm under it until he felt his love for her rekindled. On the other hand, she certainly did not wish to torment him. Love dictated that she let him know she could be a source of solace to him, not merely of irritation.

She found that he was looking at her intently, waiting to hear what she had to say. She was every bit as curious as he was to know what would issue from her mouth.

In the end, no word issued. She reached for his hand and, holding it for a moment in both of hers, put it to her lips. Abruptly, she let it go and stood. ''You pay me a great compliment, Tony, but I wish you to know

I do not regard your cousin in that way. There has been only one man I have ever regarded in that way."

He rose and said coolly, "I am bound to look after my cousin, that is all. How you regard him or anyone else is no affair of mine."

Softly, she said, "Oh, but it *is* your affair, and your taking an interest in my relations with Guy is most flattering. But there is no need to concern yourself. There has never been any reason to concern yourself."

"If I were 'concerned,' as you put it, it would hardly be surprising," he shot back. "Indeed, it would be the most natural thing in the world, given your relations with Philip Mattingly. Fortunately, however, I am not concerned, except as your behaviour affects Guy."

She took a step back, stung by his angry words.

Reaching out, he took her by the shoulders. "I have been wondering for some time what you might be plotting. If you have Guy's heart in view, I warn you to give over such thoughts. It does not matter whether you are sincere or merely amusing yourself. Either way, I will not have it."

He released her roughly, and without looking back, returned to the saloon.

When he entered, he saw that Celeste had not moved. She was as still and lovely as before. Unfortunately, the sight of her was not enough to diffuse his wrath. He was angry at Bella's cavalier tone towards his cousin. He was angry at Bella's assumption that he was as concerned about her feelings as he was about Guy's. And he was angry that, in a mockery of submissiveness, she had kissed his hand.

What angered him was the fact that Bella still had the power to plunge him into turmoil. Despite the passage of time, despite logic, reason and his affec-

tion for Celeste, he had permitted Bella to throw him
into a rage. So fiery a rage, in fact, that he was unable to utter a word. All he could do was think, and all
he could think was that if Parliament were to set him
free that very hour, it would not be soon enough.

Isabella reentered the room wearing a fixed smile
against her unusually pale complexion. Guy came
forward and entreated her to oblige him by sitting for
her likeness. Celeste seconded her brother's request
and rose from the model's chair to join Ashton. When
Isabella was seated, she noted that Ashton would not
so much as glance her way.

With his warning still fresh in her mind, she
searched Guy's face to see whether he was in any real
danger of falling in love with her. After several minutes, she was convinced that although the young man
was smitten, his case was not incurable and that
whatever she did, she would not break his heart.

Having absolved herself of attaching Guy, she was
free to think of Ashton. Part of her wished to defy him
by flirting mercilessly with Guy. Part of her wished to
be exonerated from the unjust charge of setting her
cap for a boy. In another instant, however, mortifi-
cation crowded out every other sensation. She regretted that she had kissed Ashton's hand. That had been
pure madness. She had acted on impulse, the impulse
to allay his concern, the impulse to express her true
feeling for him. After keeping herself in check for so
long, she had in one rash moment ruined everything.

At that moment, the butler announced a caller.

Ashton, who had risen from the sofa, halted at the
announcement of the name. In the entryway stood a
young man of about nineteen years of age. He looked
round the room, and when he saw that several pairs of
strange eyes greeted him, he grew ashen.

NO COST! NO OBLIGATION TO BUY!
NO PURCHASE NECESSARY!

PLAY "LUCKY 7"
AND GET AS MANY AS SIX FREE GIFTS...

HOW TO PLAY:

1. With a coin, carefully scratch off the silver box at the right. This makes you eligible to receive two or more free books, and possibly other gifts, depending on what is revealed beneath the scratch-off area.

2. You'll receive brand-new Harlequin Regency Romance™ novels. When you return this card, we'll send you the books and gifts you qualify for *absolutely free!*

3. If we don't hear from you, every other month, we'll send you 4 additional novels to read and enjoy. You can return them and owe nothing but if you decide to keep them, you'll pay only $2.69* per book, a saving of 30¢ each off the cover price. There is **no** extra charge for postage and handling. There are **no** hidden extras.

4. When you join the Harlequin Reader Service®, you'll get our subscribers'-only newsletter, as well as additional free gifts from time to time just for being a subscriber.

5. You must be completely satisfied. You may cancel at any time simply by sending us a note or a shipping statement marked ''cancel'' or by returning any shipment to us at our cost.

This lovely heart-shaped box is richly detailed with cut-glass decorations, perfect for holding a precious memento or keepsake—and it's yours absolutely free when you accept our no-risk offer.

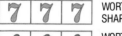

**Just scratch off the silver box with a coin.
Then check below to see which gifts you get.**

YES! I have scratched off the silver box. Please send me all the gifts for which I qualify. I understand I am under no obligation to purchase any books, as explained on the opposite page.

248 CIH AEL9
(U-H-RG-05/92)

NAME

ADDRESS   APT

CITY   STATE   ZIP

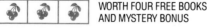

WORTH FOUR FREE BOOKS, FREE HEART-
SHAPED GLASS BOX AND MYSTERY BONUS

WORTH FOUR FREE BOOKS
AND MYSTERY BONUS

WORTH THREE FREE BOOKS

WORTH TWO FREE BOOKS

HARLEQUIN "NO RISK" GUARANTEE

- You're not required to buy a single book—ever!
- You must be completely satisfied or you may cancel at any time simply by sending us a note or a shipping statement marked "cancel" or returning any shipment to us at our cost. Either way, you will receive no more books; you'll have no obligation to buy.
- The free books and gifts you receive from this "Lucky 7" offer remain yours to keep no matter what you decide.

If offer card is missing, write to: Harlequin Reader Service, 3010 Walden Ave., P.O. Box 1867, Buffalo, NY 14269-1867

Celeste whispered in Ashton's ear. "Who is he?"

He appeared not to have heard.

She placed a delicate hand on his arm, saying, "The poor gentleman is dreadfully uneasy."

Ashton made no reply.

"His face is kind," she whispered.

He looked at the visitor.

"And handsome, too."

That observation provoked him to reply. "One never regards as handsome," he said sternly, "the face of one's enemy."

PART THREE

Antiquities, Rarities and Curiosities

CHAPTER ELEVEN

"IT IS CHAD!" Tassie exclaimed. "I have been saying to Bella these three days now that he might come down from Oxford. I expressly said that as soon as he could get away, he would come to us. But nobody regards anything I say. I am less than nothing."

The others closely observed the young man, who seemed to hesitate to step forward. They saw Isabella rush to greet him and permit him to kiss her cheek. The two exchanged a few whispered words which brought a shine to Isabella's eyes and a tentative smile to the young man's lips. Celeste whispered to Ashton that the young man must be a near relation, so intimate was the footing on which he seemed in that household.

Tassie approached to say, "Bella will bring him to you in a moment. She will want to introduce Chad Mattingly to your acquaintance."

Ashton flicked an invisible speck from the lapel of his coat, then looked up to regard the son of Philip Mattingly.

Tassie's prediction was borne out: Isabella brought the young man to be presented. The affection in her voice was undisguised. As Chad murmured shy greetings to the strangers, Ashton found his resemblance to his father disturbing. However, his manners did not resemble his father's. The boy was as diffident as a maiden and could scarcely look him in the eye.

Celeste smiled encouragement at Chad, but as he
was wholly unable to contemplate such loveliness as
she represented, he did not respond.

Seeing that the newcomer was ill at ease, Guy offered him one or two quiet, inconsequential remarks.
These unexceptionable observations on the weather,
the journey from Oxford and the cosiness of the present gathering caused Chad to respond with the first
audible words he had uttered since his entrance. He
went so far as to answer Guy in a complete sentence.

Isabella cast Guy a grateful look, which spurred the
young Canadian to intensify his efforts to draw Chad
out. It soon developed that the two shared a passion
for the races. When Chad mentioned that a much
talked of specimen of superior horseflesh was sched-
uled to appear at Tattersall's and that he had come
down for the purpose of inspecting it, Guy declared he
was eager to view the animal. Would Mr. Mattingly
permit him to accompany him? Yes, indeed, Mr.
Mattingly would be pleased. Thus, it was settled.

Ashton was invited to join their party, as he would
no doubt wish to add to his stable if he meant to make
any stay in London. But he declined; he was engaged
to Mr. Doty, he said firmly.

WHEN ASHTON VISITED the law chambers on the following day, he heard with pleasure that Mr. Doty had
begun to draft a petition for a private bill of divorce.

"This is excellent news," Ashton said. "I had not
expected matters to go forward so speedily."

"Ah," said the lawyer, "the public has the notion
that the wheels of justice turn slowly. I take no offence at such a notion, first, because it is no less than
the truth, and, second, because its slowness is, in my
view, one of the chief virtues of English law. Men who

rush to sue or to dispute or, dare I say it, to divorce, may repent of it later. Happily, the law gives them months, years, even decades in which to mull things over and change their minds."

"I do not propose to change my mind," Ashton assured him. "I wish to proceed with all due haste."

"Very well. We shall now seek through the Common Law Courts a verdict of damages for criminal conversation against your wife's seducer."

Ashton folded his arms. "That will not be necessary."

"But you must present such a verdict in support of the divorce petition. And surely you wish to see the man pay for what he cost you in conjugal felicity."

"I trust he has paid. He is dead."

"Excellent. His being dead will prove an acceptable circumstance explaining the absence of such a verdict. As the Roman sage has said, 'Dead men cannot bite.'"

Ashton did not smile at this salient wit.

"As it is not necessary to pursue the verdict in the Civil Courts, all that remains is to await the decree from the Ecclesiastical Courts and to hunt up the witnesses. Their depositions shall be presented before Parliament as proof of the adultery. Happily, there are always witnesses aplenty to oblige in such cases. In my experience, they always have much to say, and what they do not absolutely know, they are more than willing to invent."

Ashton's fingers closed around the arms of his chair. He regarded Mr. Doty with distaste.

"We shall need to gather every fact we can discover," Mr. Doty went on cheerily, "not merely dates and times and specific circumstances, but details as well. It is the details—stained sheets, love letters and the like—which lend best support to a petition for divorce.''

A thundercloud appeared on Ashton's face. He stood, walked to the grimy window which looked out upon the inns of the district and clasped his hands behind his back.

"If you do not know of any witnesses," Mr. Doty said, "we shall set an investigator to discovering some. Servants always have a great deal of evidence to offer in such cases, and while some of them may keep mum out of a misguided loyalty, most will speak the truth at last and provide all the particulars.''

Barely containing his revulsion, Ashton said, "Do you seriously propose to interview servants in connection with this matter?''

"Oh, I am quite accustomed to it, I assure you. Servants have excellent memories, especially in cases of adultery. They never forget the creepings along the stairways, the promises and quarrels overheard, the assignations at midnight, the quantities of champagne consumed, the noisy quarrels and the rumpled condition of the bed the following morning.''

Ashton breathed hard. His wrath seemed in danger of exploding, but after a time, the thundercloud dissipated and a cold, steely glint replaced it. He affected a granite calm, saying, "What you suggest is singularly vile.''

"The law does not concern itself with what is vile. It is concerned only with what may be legally done. Interviewing witnesses, taking their depositions and presenting the evidence in the House of Commons are not only proper legal methods but they are the prescribed procedures for obtaining what you seek. Unless your wife is proved to be an adulteress, you cannot obtain a bill of divorce.''

"I see. So one is required to be vile, in your view. Well, I am not persuaded."

"If I may be permitted to say, sir, your scruples may add to the difficulty of the case. Difficult cases drag on for years and years. On the other hand, time may work in your favour. I suppose Mrs. Ashton cannot live forever."

"It occurs to me, Mr. Doty, that the law encourages vice. It renders divorce so hideous that the least disgusting course is to resign oneself to taking a mistress or a lover."

Pleased, Mr. Doty said, "I am thankful you understand how it is."

"I do not understand, Mr. Doty, and I do not intend to."

"Eh?"

"You will proceed in a manner which is not vile, and if you cannot devise one, I shall be obliged to seek another solicitor."

Swallowing hard, the lawyer nodded quickly. "I take my oath, sir, I shall be the soul of discretion. I beg pardon if I offended you."

"You shall conduct the business as quietly as may be. The witnesses whose depositions you hear shall be interviewed in complete privacy. You are to interview them personally, and their evidence is to be confined to times and dates and circumstances. Details they happen to provide are not to be made fodder for gossips. Do you take my meaning?"

Mr. Doty lowered his eyes. "If I had any doubts before, sir, I believe you have sufficiently clarified them. There will be no need for you to seek another attorney. Everything shall be exactly as you wish."

THAT AFTERNOON, Ashton received a note from Celeste informing him that Chad Mattingly had offered to take them all to Madame Tussaud's and requesting that he join them. It appeared that she longed to see the waxworks.

He smiled to think how charmingly she would exclaim over the figures, but, for himself, he declined. After sending off a messenger with his regrets, he set off for Candover. He had to meet again with his steward, reacquaint himself with the tenants, discover what food and other shortages the county suffered owing to the war and observe whether the hops and oats prospered. As he was needful of vigorous exercise and fresh air to dispel the effects of his visit to Mr. Doty, he set off on horseback.

The ride refreshed him. He took pleasure in the spring breeze, the clouds bulging against the blue sky and the rolling countryside patched in shades of green and gold. When he reached the village of Wordham, only a mile from Candover, he stopped to admire the neat shops and houses he had known as a youth. At the church of St. Michael's, where several generations of Ashtons were buried, he dismounted. The family vault, where William lay, was in a corner of the church.

After tethering his horse, he entered the path under the peaked wooden arch. Elms lined the way to the church door. The spire looked purple against the puffy clouds. There was no one about. Opening the church door, he saw it was dark and empty inside.

It took him a moment to adjust his eyes to the subdued light filtering from the high arched windows. Walking down the aisle between the pews, he approached the nave, at the far end of which the Ashton vault was located. While he walked, he took in the absolute stillness of the church, unbroken but for the whisper of his footsteps.

Abruptly, a hooded figure rose from one of the front pews and approached a monument in the wall. The figure paused for a considerable time, then touched the monument with a gloved hand. He recognized the monument, for it was William's, and he recognized the hooded figure as well, for it was Bella.

CHAPTER TWELVE

ISABELLA HAD COME THERE, as she often came, to remember. Her habit was to sit for an hour and allow meditation to mingle with scattered thoughts of William. At these times, she allowed herself the luxury of tears. Engrossed in her musings, she had not heard the echo of steps on the stone floor. She was not aware of another presence in the church until she placed her hand upon the monument.

Thinking the rector had come in, she drew her hand away and turned. She froze at the sight of Ashton looking at her starkly. Because the church was dark and an eerie brightness fell from the high, ancient windows, he appeared an apparition. A moment later, she knew he was real, for he came to her, pulled her to him and buried his face in her hair.

When he released her, she stepped back to see his face. Too surprised by his appearance to be conscious of her tears, she did not wipe them from her face.

He led her to a pew, where she sat. Then he sat—and so near to her that their shoulders touched. They said nothing for a considerable time until she whispered, "Do you remember when I gave him his bath?"

"As I recall, it was you who ended by being bathed."

"Very true."

"I also recall that he was laughing, wilful and charming, like his mother."

"He was determined and brave, like his father."

"Well, you will agree that he was ill-tempered when crossed, like his grandfather."

She smiled. "Yes, he was, but was incomparably sweet, like no one else."

He remained silent.

"Perhaps you think I am too partial," she said. "I suppose I may be. All mothers and fathers believe that their offspring are the sweetest, most precocious, well formed and delightful creatures who ever trod the Earth."

"You are not too partial, in my view. Those facts were indisputably true of William."

"I never thought to hear you speak of him."

"I never have spoken of him, until now."

ONE WOULD HAVE THOUGHT, when the heavy oak church door swung open, that they were a bridal couple. Both smiled as they emerged into the April sunshine. He stopped, turned to her with a slight bow and offered his arm. She favoured him with a graceful curtsy, placed her hand on his arm and they stepped onto the path to the church gate.

Even though they were not a bridal couple, they were an attractive pair. A dark blue coat and fawn pantaloons accentuated his height, while a hint of early grey at his temples enhanced his natural dignity. Removing her cloak, Isabella revealed a military-style scarlet spencer with bugle trim and gold buttons. These were complemented by a white skirt and a scarlet silk hat with a delicate matching feather. The brilliant colour of her ensemble heightened her animation. He put on his black beaver and led her along the elm-lined path.

The quiet quarter hour in the church had worked a change. Each had spoken William's name. Each had let the other glimpse the grief that had before been hidden. Each understood for the first time that the other grieved as painfully. Speaking, revealing and understanding had lifted a weight from their spirits.

At the gate, they turned into the high street of the town. The first shop they came to was a tobacconist's, where Isabella purchased a quantity of snuff for her grandfather. Until his mixture arrived from Sharrow, she said, the old rogue was always looking for something to do with his nose and too often what he did was poke it into her business. Next they entered the linen-draper's shop. There Anthony bought a card of lace for Tassie, who no doubt had thought nobody would mind what she said when she expressed a strong desire for black trimming. Afterwards, they took some refreshment at the White Stag and talked of the lilacs at Candover, which were in leaf, the horse-chestnuts, which were quite out, and the flower border of the pinks and sweet-william along the gravel drive, which were to be planted. Their conversation flowed like that of a couple engrossed in the cheerful details of domestic life.

When they left the White Stag, they were met by a servant who informed Isabella that the carriage waited to return her to London. Ashton might have handed her to the carriage, but the events of the afternoon had been such that he could not let her go. "You cannot leave now," he said. "You must give me a tour of the churchyard."

"The colonies must be fearfully dull if you look to entertain yourself in churchyards," she replied. But because she treasured the new understanding they had reached and because she did not wish to leave him so soon, she gave instructions to have the horses walked up and down for a bit.

Returning to the church gate, they entered the grounds of St. Michael's.

"Where shall we begin?" Isabella asked. "With the Pettibills, I think. Yes, they always have the liveliest epitaphs."

The churchyard lay in the shadow of the jasper-walled church. Its old gravestones were weatherworn and tipped every which way but straight. They passed among the stones in the gentle spring air, and whenever Ashton noticed a familiar name and a recent date, he stopped. Isabella, who regularly visited the neighbourhood, gave him the information he required concerning the family of the deceased, whether they were in want and what might be done by the master of Candover to relieve their difficulties.

"And now you have all the facts," she concluded, "or nearly all."

"Nearly? I thought your history most complete. What more can there be to tell?"

She turned to him and, taking a breath for courage, said, "I wish you to know the truth of what happened with Philip Mattingly."

He stiffened. "I do not ask for explanations. I never have."

"I know. I wish you had. I wish you had evinced the slightest curiosity."

"It sours a man's taste for information to learn that his wife loves another man and means to live with him."

"But you do not know all the facts."

His jawline hardened. He paused, then said in a collected tone, "You evidently wish to tell me what you call 'the facts,' but, be assured, they are a matter of indifference to me."

She refused to be provoked by this reflection, saying only, "Do you recollect what you did after William died?"

"I remember nothing of that time."

"Allow me to tell you, then. The first thing you did was to travel to Scotland. Do you recall?"

"Yes, now you mention it. I went hunting."

"It is an odd thing to do, I think, to assuage one's sorrow by shooting grouse."

He regarded her closely. "I see what you are hinting at. You were piqued because I spent a fortnight at my lodge."

"No, I merely wish you had understood my feelings."

"And I wish you had understood mine. A man who has just lost his son must do something with himself, however ridiculous."

"A woman who has lost her son must do something, as well. I wanted you by my side."

"Did you? I do not remember it quite that way. As I recollect, you sat day after day, holding his sleeping gown and looking out the window. You scarcely noticed my comings and goings and would not speak to me at all. You were too engrossed in your own sorrow to notice mine. I had never known you to be so still and silent. After a period, I could not go on watching you, and so I went hunting."

"You said you had forgotten that time."

"I remember that I could do no more for you than I had been able to do for William."

Emotion caused her voice to quaver. "Neither of us could do anything for William, nor for each other. I suppose that is why you left Scotland to go sailing on Lord Grosbeak's yacht.''

"I scarcely know what I did, let alone why I did it. I only know that I have always detested sailing. Even more, I have always detested Lord Grosbeak.''

"And yet you went,'' she said. "And when you grew weary of doing what you detested, you went to Ireland to fish. You would go anywhere, it seemed, but where I was.''

"You might have written to say you wanted me to come.''

"I was afraid you would not.''

"I would have come instantly.''

"I was too proud to ask.''

He levelled a half smile at her. "I see what you have in view. You wish to impress upon me the fact that Mattingly was on the spot, while I was off sporting. That is your excuse for everything which followed.''

"You misconstrue my meaning. I do not blame you.''

"Of course not. You merely say that because I disported myself on land and sea, you decided to run off. It is all perfectly rational. Any wife would have done the same.''

"That is not how it was.''

"Very well,'' he said with icy calm, "tell me how it was.''

Fear welled in her a moment but she put it aside. She walked quickly to the shade of the yew, where he caught up to her, stopping close to her shoulder. Scolding herself for cowardice, she said breathlessly, "When the doctor told me that William's fever was very bad, I did not believe him. I recollect telling you at the time that you did not need to fret; the child would certainly be well again. After all, I reasoned, calamity would not dare to befall a Wortwell. It certainly would not befall *me*. I had never been thwarted in anything. I had always been given everything I ever wanted.

"My foolishness was brought home to me the night you carried him from his bed to his coffin. I have never forgotten how tiny he looked, how tiny and stiff. When I felt his cheek, it was as cold as those gravestones. For the first time, I knew that no amount of wilfulness on my part would bring him back.

"I felt humbled, Tony. All the time we were mourning him, I saw clearly how it was with wives. I had imagined that our lives were taken up with being coddled, fondled and spoiled. My view of woman's lot greatly resembled my view of childhood, for toys, silliness and having one's way played the principal roles. When William died, I saw that, in fact, we wives must spend a good deal of our lives bearing and burying children. Of the wives I knew who had borne children, not one had seen above half live to the age of five.

"You know me too well to imagine that I have ever doubted myself, but I doubted then. I doubted whether I was brave enough, sensible enough or good enough to endure what a wife must endure. In my uncertainty, I looked to you to tell me that I was better than I thought I was. But when I looked for you, you were hunting grouse and yachting with Grosbeak."

At this, he looked at her sharply. "I do not deny I was full of myself and my woe. I do not deny I wanted only to distance myself from both. I do not deny any of it. Is that what you wished to hear, Bella? Well, now you have heard it. Does that vindicate you? Do you feel justified at last?" Taking her by the shoulders, he turned her round so that he could see her eyes.

She shielded them with her hand, unable to withstand his scrutiny. "I do not flatter myself that I can justify. But I can explain. You see, Philip befriended me. To him I spoke of William, describing his little ways, laughing and weeping as the feeling dictated. Philip had an inexhaustible fund of patience."

"And he profited mightily by it."

She could not ignore this hit. "He came by his patience painfully, I assure you. His wife was acutely ill. She had been given a death warrant by the doctors. She had been given several such warrants, in fact. Yet she hung on, always getting a little worse, but never bearing out the physicians' prophecies that she would be dead within the week. In this manner, they had lived for some years, and as difficult as it was for Philip, it was even worse for his son."

"Do not catalogue Philip Mattingly's difficulties to me, if you please."

She took a breath to steady herself, determined not to be goaded, searching for a way of telling the truth so that he would believe it. "I do not ask you to sympathize with Philip's situation. I merely wish to explain about Chad. He was a boy of fifteen or sixteen and to all intents and purposes a motherless boy. I was a childless mother. Angry though you are, Tony, surely you can imagine what my feelings were."

"And so you undertook to fill the office of mother to him. Very charitable of you, I'm sure. Do go on."

"Shortly after you left for Canada, the same fever that had taken William took Philip. Within the space of a few months, I lost child, husband and friend. Yet Philip's wife, who had lingered on the point of death for years, continued to live."

"The irony did not escape you, I trust."

"No, it did not. I might have fared better if I had been one of those females who swoons or produces a fountain of tears as frequently as she takes tea. However, my fate is to see irony and to laugh at it and so, naturally, everybody thought I had lost my wits, for I often found myself laughing in the most solemn settings—principally at church and the opera. Disgusted at my behaviour, Grandpapa whisked me off to Wortwell, as if one could recover one's wits in that dreary, ghost-ridden palace.

"What restored me was not the change of scene but the death of Philip's wife. The only provision made for Chad was an annuity which was to pay for his board at school and university. As to family and connections, there were none who could be persuaded to take an interest in the boy. Even if there had been, he would not willingly have gone to them, for he had become attached to me. Of course, I could not by law become his guardian, but I did, in fact, take on that responsibility, and it required that I cease nursing my sorrows and tend to the business of raising a young gentleman. Since that time, Chad's home has been in Hertford Street; whenever he has come down from school or university, he has come to me."

"That is a most illuminating explanation," he said. "Your desire to unburden yourself of all the facts is now satisfied, I trust, and I shall make so bold as to suggest that you not keep your horses waiting another moment. They have been walked too long as it is. I shall take you to your carriage."

He tipped his hat and would have led her to the gate but she seized his arm. "Stay, Tony. There is more."

"There is no need for more. I understand perfectly. Your husband took a lengthy vacation and therefore you took a lover. What could be more natural?"

Helpless, she cried, "I never loved Philip Mattingly."

He treated her to the ironic smile which was his hallmark. "If you intended to elope with him without loving him," he said, "then you are greatly to be pitied."

She bowed her head.

He summoned her servant to bring the carriage round and then, with a click of his heels, he left her. As she watched his sure progress towards the gate, oppression overwhelmed her. She would never, it seemed, have the opportunity to disclose the secret which stood between them.

On his side there was a similar disquiet. All the harmony their shared grief had established was now destroyed. Though the Atlantic no longer separated them, he and Bella could not have been further apart.

CHAPTER THIRTEEN

CHAD MATTINGLY was not only a student of ancient languages and history, but something of an archaeologist, geologist and naturalist, as well. These scholarly passions had secured him a recommendation from the dean of his college to Mr. Joseph Planta, Principal Librarian of the British Museum. The young man was to be admitted to the Reading Room to peruse the DaCosta collection of Hebrew Biblical manuscripts. In addition, he was given permission to view the natural history collections and, in particular, the discoveries of Captain Cook.

As soon as Guy DuChateau learned of the rare privilege to which his new young friend was to be admitted, he too wished to obtain a ticket to the exhibits. Guy and his sister were seated in the blue saloon in Hertford Street when Chad alluded to his intention to make a pilgrimage to the Museum. The young Canadian said that he had heard with interest of the wondrous treasures on display in Montague House. He had never had the pleasure of visiting a truly great museum, unless Madame Tussaud's waxworks might be considered one, and had read that the British Museum housed not only a cyclops pig but also a horn from the head of a most unfortunate woman, whose portrait, showing both horns, hung nearby. Nothing, Guy declared, could be more entertaining than to see such prodigies with one's own eyes.

Celeste could not help overhearing her brother's enquiries on the subject, and it was not long before she too conceived a great desire to see the antiquities, rarities and curiosities gathered at Montague House. Because the public hours were limited, and because the Reading Room was open only to those who could produce a recommendation from a person of known character, the young people applied to Isabella, hoping she might use her connections to gain them admission.

She laughed, declaring that no one would ever mistake her for a person of known character, but she did at last confess that one of the Trustees nursed a tendre for her and on the strength of that, she might procure them tickets.

She had just settled down to write to the amorous Trustee when Ashton was announced. For some days, he had declined to join his cousins on their visits to Hertford Street, feeling that his last encounter with Bella needed to fade a little from memory before he could be easy in her company once more. He had come on this occasion to fetch Celeste to Lady Pillowbank's. Isabella, who had surmised the reason for his recent absence, coloured when he entered the saloon.

She was spared the necessity of speaking to him by Celeste, who informed him in a rapturous tone of the projected excursion. Tassie, who was pinning to a dress the black lace Ashton had bought her, asked him if he was not perishing to view the Egyptian mummies, for which the Museum was renowned.

"You know, Tony," she exclaimed, "one trembles to think that Bonaparte's armies might have carried off each and every one of those mummies! How fortunate it is that we saved them from falling into French hands."

"I should so like to see them," Celeste murmured to Ashton. "I hope you will make one of the party, cousin. You will come, won't you?"

Isabella peered studiously at Tassie's pinnings, prepared to hear Ashton decline.

But he smiled at Celeste, saying indulgently, "I shall accompany you, if it will please you. As one has to travel only as far as Bloomsbury to view such wonders, one might as well have a look."

"Oh, that is what I hoped you'd say," Celeste cried. "I have heard that the mummies are spectacular."

"If you like mummies," Isabella remarked, "you are sure to love the vulture's head in spirits and the stuffed flamingo also on display."

"I shall like them above all things," the girl agreed.

Isabella was then prevailed upon to write for the tickets, which she was more than anxious to do now that Ashton had decided to join their party. That he no longer sought to avoid her company gave her a glimmer of hope. Calling for pen and paper, she dashed off a note to the Trustee, and was then left alone with Tassie to await the answer. Within hours, a servant brought a reply: a letter recommending the entire party to the care of Mr. Taylor Combe, Keeper of Coins and Metals, who would put them in the hands of the proper officers.

On the following day, they set out for Bloomsbury in a capacious curricle of which, Ashton informed them all, he was the new owner. He brought with him his cousins and regrets from Wild Goose, who had promised to entertain the Old Duke by interpreting his dreams.

The day was fine, permitting them to ride under the open sky until they were set down at the Museum gatehouse. There they paused to admire the brightly uniformed soldiers charged with protecting the nation's collectibles against defilement by the public. Mr. Combe came out to greet them and take them into the hall. They climbed the elegant scrollwork staircase, admired the gaily decorated walls and were then conducted along the passage.

They reached the Reading Room, which was filled with scholars sitting at the long tables in various attitudes of study. Accommodation was found for the party at a corner table by a tall window, and when they had arranged themselves comfortably, Mr. Combe caused several books to be brought. Chad overcame his shyness long enough to explain that the ancient volumes had been acquired by Charles II from a philanthropist named DaCosta. Then, having shown each and every one the royal cipher on the covers, he sat down, opened to the first page of the first book and became engrossed in reading. As the others did not understand Hebrew, it did not take them long to weary of admiring the gilt illustrations. Soon they began to distract themselves with looking about and yawning.

At last, relief came in the person of Mr. Combe. Isabella asked him if they might begin their tour of the Egyptian hall. Glad to oblige, he bowed them out of the Reading Room. Chad, who wished to continue his study of the Hebrew texts, and Celeste, who wished to learn more of the ancient language which fascinated Chad, remained behind.

In the gallery, the objects displayed caused Tassie to gasp. Enormous heads of pharaohs loomed over them as they moved down the aisle. Sarcophagi many times the size of a human carcass lined the wall. Inside the

sarcophagi, she knew, lay the mummies, who might
rise from their coffins at any moment to give them all
a dreadful fright. She tugged Ashton's arm, whisper-
ing that the ancient Egyptians had done things on
rather too grand a scale to be quite elegant, but he did
not hear. He was preoccupied with observing Isabella
and Guy, who walked ahead together, and he did not
like what he saw.

It was apparent to him that Guy admired Isabella
more than ever. He saw the young man touch her elbow at two opportunities. Even now, he was fussing
over her comfort and hanging on her words. He hov-
ered in such a way that nobody else could get near her.

Still more provoking was Isabella's conduct. Instead of giving Guy a set-down, she smiled at him and
his sallies. She stood with him at the box which displayed the Rosetta Stone, trying to imagine what the
hieroglyphics said and laughing when Guy insisted
that the words were those of a love letter. Ashton
could not hear precisely what they said, but the word
love was perfectly distinct. Clearly, in spite of his tête-
à-tête with Isabella at Hertford Street, she had not
given up her plot to ensnare Guy.

"Do you suppose this can really be the sarcopha-
gus of Alexander the Great?" Tassie asked him as she
pondered a stone coffin of monstrous proportions.

Alexander be damned, he thought. He could not
stand idly by, watching Isabella's behaviour, and do
nothing.

Tassie detained him over the question of where they
would find the Magna Carta. It must be in another
gallery; it would certainly not be lodged with the
mummies, she declared.

Absently, Ashton nodded. Then, looking up, he saw
that Guy and Isabella had disappeared. He glanced

round quickly but found them nowhere, though they had been in his sights a moment ago. The officer in whose hands Mr. Combe had placed them gazed placidly at a carved pillar, unaware that two members of his party had left his care. Apart from the guide, Tassie and Ashton, no other live human creature inhabited the gallery.

GUY PEEKED into an anteroom hidden from view by a marble column. Finding it empty of everything except dusty manuscripts, he invited Isabella to explore it with him.

She declined, saying that the room must be private. In point of fact, she did not wish to lose sight of Ashton. She had hopes of seeing an exchange of partners which would place her at his side instead of his cousin's. This outing, she feared, might be her only opportunity to put things right. In all likelihood, she and Ashton would never quite restore the good understanding they had come to at William's monument, but the recollection of that precious intimacy must still have been as fresh in his mind as it was in hers. If so, they might be able to regain a modicum of their former civility.

Guy whispered that he had something particular to say to her and that it could not wait another moment. As he appeared uncharacteristically serious, Isabella relented, and on the proviso that they would stay only a moment, she went inside.

Despite his avowed desire to confide in her, as soon as she entered, Guy began to inspect the manuscripts, blowing on them to create clouds of dust and peering at their strange writing as though one could comprehend it by dint of squinting.

"What did you wish to say to me, Mr. Du-Chateau?" she asked.

"I believe I have found Cleopatra's diary," he said. "Come and have a look. I vow, it looks a scandalous thing."

She eyed him sceptically, then declared that she would return to the others.

"One moment, if you please," he said, and coming to her with three long strides, he took her in his arms and kissed her.

Caught off guard, Isabella did not move. When at last she recovered her senses, she would have pushed him from her, but the sound of a throat clearing caused Guy to release her.

In the entrance stood Ashton. He said nothing but looked everything. Before Guy could speak, Tassie appeared in the doorway and asked, "Why, whatever is the matter?"

The first to find voice was Isabella, who read anger in Ashton's expression. Alarmed, she moved to Tassie, took her by the arm and announced that they must hurry and see the Portland vase. On that, the two ladies went into the hall where they were quickly lost to view.

Left alone, the gentlemen made no move to leave. With a grin, Guy said, "You have found me out, so I might as well confess it, Tony, I admire Mrs. Ashton more than I can say. I hope you will not be offended. My liking her does not make me value your friendship any the less."

Ashton came inside and closed the door.

"The truth is," Guy said, "I mean to do you an immense favour. I shall take her off your hands so that you will not be troubled with her support."

"Give up this nonsense," Ashton said.

Affronted, Guy replied, "I do not consider it non-sense and I will not give it up."

"You are too young. You do not know what you are doing."

"Ask Isabella whether I am too young!"

"You are too young to realize the harm you are do-ing."

"That is my concern, and I will thank you not to interfere."

"Bella is my concern, and what does harm to her is my concern, as well."

"You speak as though you meant to defend her honour instead of divorce her!"

A thundercloud transformed Ashton's face.

Ashamed of having broken his promise to be silent, Guy explained, "Bella told me everything. She did not mean to let it slip. She could not help herself."

"I am obliged to tell you that Bella's reputation is endangered by your infamous conduct. A gentleman does not kiss a lady in a museum or any other public place without subjecting her to the worst sort of gos-sip."

"I trust that you alone witnessed the kiss, and I never heard that you were fond of blabbing. By the same token, nothing pleases Isabella so well as incit-ing gossip."

"I do not speak of general gossip. I speak of what will be brought against her for the purposes of the divorce. Bella's every move may be construed as evi-dence. Mr. Doty wishes to seek witnesses every-where—perhaps even in the hallowed halls of mu-seums—to unearth evidence of misconduct."

Reddening, Guy said, "I would never harm her."

"You have already harmed her. It is one thing to be subjected to testimony in regard to events which took place years ago. It is quite another to hear publicly revealed the most intimate details of what is even now taking place."

Guy looked remorseful. "I give you my word, Tony. Henceforth, I shall kiss her only in private."

This avowal satisfied Ashton not at all. "You will keep your distance from her or answer to me," he said. On that, he left the young man alone, surrounded by stacks of dusty, indecipherable manuscripts.

ISABELLA AND TASSIE sought out the Museum officer, who was kind enough to escort them to the Portland vase. He had just traced its history as far as the wealthy Barberini family in the previous century, when Isabella, pleading a headache, excused herself. Before Tassie could fuss, Isabella ran off, making her way through a maze of halls, rooms and stairways. At last, she found the entrance to the courtyard. Outside, she breathed deeply of the late spring air and endeavoured to calm herself. Seating herself on the marble bench beneath an acacia, she saw again the expression on Ashton's face when he had found her in the arms of Guy DuChateau. It was not unlike what she had witnessed at Covent Garden. It mirrored some deep trouble, and she was no better able to solace him now than she had been then, or for that matter, when William had died.

Humbly, achingly, she concluded that her plan had failed. She had not been able to make Tony love her again and she never would. If she had not dreaded to hear Tassie's cries and moans, she would have run to her that instant, placed her head on her powdery bosom and wept. As it was, she was obliged to weep alone, which she would have proceeded to do with force had not Ashton come into the courtyard then.

Because he had been searching for her some time, he felt a grim satisfaction at discovering her. The fragrance of the acacia's spraying white flowers caused him to slow a little in his determined pace. He saw that her face was shaded by the purple bonnet she wore, but her green, glistening eyes were clearly visible.

CHAPTER FOURTEEN

"DO NOT SCOLD ME, Tony," she said in a subdued voice. "You were right; I was mistaken about Mr. DuChateau. I had no idea of his being so besotted. He seemed such a sensible boy."

He stood by the bench and regarded her seriously. "I was obliged to speak to him."

"I hope you did not scold him very harshly. He is a dear boy, for all his impetuosity."

Frowning, he said, "Perhaps I have been at fault. I ought to have told you sooner what is at stake."

Heartsick, she looked at her hands in her lap.

"As you know, Bella, your conduct is under the severest scrutiny."

"I'm afraid the Town never wearies of chattering of my exploits. I vow, I have all I can do to invent outrages worthy of their notice."

He shook his head. "It is not the Town I speak of, but the lawyers. They will listen to anybody who is willing to take his oath that you were spied in the British Museum kissing a gentleman."

"What does it matter what nasty rumours lawyers and such creatures choose to put about?"

"How can I impress upon you the disastrous results which must follow from a flirtation with Guy DuChateau? Not only must it end badly for you both, but the talk it will excite must turn you into a figure of ridicule."

Sighing, she smiled gently. "Are you endeavouring to reform my ways, Tony? Think what would happen if I should suddenly conduct myself like a saint: the Town would perish with boredom, and you would have to answer for it."

He determined to speak plainly so that she would be serious. "Bella, I do not refer to mere gossip. Everything you do may be considered material to the divorce."

"The divorce?" She recoiled as though a snake had hissed at her.

He studied her ashen face.

To prevent his seeing her brimming eyes, she turned her head away. Making one last desperate attempt, she said, "I know that you do not wish us to live as husband and wife, Tony, but I do not see, I have never seen, why you insist upon bringing Mr. Doty into our affairs. We have agreed to be civil, have we not? Can we not continue as we are? Such arrangements are common. It is unnecessary to go to the trouble of divorce when we may go on being perfectly cosy."

Obliged to confess the truth, he said, "It is not possible, Bella. I wish to be free to remarry."

She gazed at him in astonishment.

"Until the divorce is decreed, I am not at liberty to speak, but as soon as I am, I intend to ask Miss DuChateau for her hand in marriage."

Isabella put her fingertips to her lips. She imagined she saw Celeste's madonnalike face. The girl's virtues also rose in her mind; she was everything a respectable gentleman would wish to have in a wife. Although Isabella sat in the fresh spring air, she felt stifled.

"I see by your expression," he said, "that you are shocked. No doubt you are thinking of the disparity in our ages and interests. I have considered that, and I believe that Celeste and I shall suit. She is a mild, fragile girl in need of a protector. I am a man alone, ready and willing to protect.''

Isabella contrived to steady her voice and reply, ''I do not wonder that you wish to marry her. Any man would.''

''You are aware, I know, that in order for a man to obtain a bill of divorce, evidence must be presented of his wife's faithlessness. To provide such evidence, the lawyers are obliged to scour the nation for witnesses. No servant, however lowly, no acquaintance, however remote, is considered too insignificant. I have instructed Mr. Doty to proceed discreetly and to prevent gossip wherever possible. Nevertheless, he will view testimony as to your present behaviour no less incriminating than the evidence regarding your relations with Philip Mattingly.''

''He is seeking evidence in regard to Philip?'' she cried.

''Naturally. You knew he would.''

Aghast, she stood. ''I did not think it would ever come to this—to the point of hunting up witnesses and hearing testimony. I believed we would reach an understanding before such action was taken. Oh, this is dreadful, dreadful.''

''I could not agree more. But I shall do what I can to ensure Mr. Doty's discretion.''

''I care nothing for discretion. Scandal does not frighten me. But I do fear the outcome if Mr. Doty continues his search for evidence.''

''Why?''

''Because there is no evidence. There is no testimony. There is no servant, no acquaintance who can swear to my relations with Philip Mattingly.''

"Mr. Doty has sworn to look under every rock in Britain, if he must."

"You do not understand. There were no relations, at least not of the kind which will be useful to you. I am so sorry to have to tell you this, Tony. Once again, I have ruined everything. You will be unable to obtain a divorce, unable to marry Celeste and you will never forgive me, I know."

"Calm yourself, Bella. You are scarcely intelligible."

"You must stop Mr. Doty at once. You must go to him without delay, for when he questions witnesses, he will learn that Philip Mattingly was never my lover!" Unable to endure the sight of his disappointment, she hurried from the courtyard and did not look back.

WHEN ASHTON WENT to collect the others a quarter of an hour later, he learned that Isabella had caused one of the Museum officers to summon a hack so that she might be carried home. Tassie recollected that her cousin had complained of a violent headache and had been compelled to forgo the history of the Portland vase so that she might get some air. On hearing this news, Chad and Celeste worried that Isabella was gravely ill, while Guy declared that there could be no pleasure in any museum, however fine, without Mrs. Ashton.

Throughout the conversation, Ashton remained silent. Isabella's outburst had stunned him. She had said—or blurted out, rather—a contradiction of everything she had proclaimed two years earlier. Having taken her at her word then, he was now to believe the complete opposite. He could scarcely absorb her meaning, but if what she appeared to be saying was to be believed, the consequences would be far-reaching.

As she had rightly foreseen, he would not have the grounds to obtain a divorce. He would never be free to marry Celeste. Instead, he would remain married to a woman who, for some reason known only to herself, had been determined to make him to think her an adulteress.

At Hertford Street, Isabella was denied to all callers. To enquiries, the footman shrugged, repeated "Her ladyship is not receiving," and rolled his eyes.

It was thought that Chad might be admitted to her sitting-room, for Isabella's fondness for the young man was proverbial, but, upon trial, this expectation proved incorrect.

"She would not open the door to me and refuses to see anyone at all," Chad confided to the others. "I hope she is not prostrate with illness."

"Madam is in a state," the footman whispered to Tassie, who, much to her chagrin, had also been excluded from Isabella's sight. The instant the others left the house, taking Chad with them, Tassie repaired to Isabella's sitting-room, which she found locked against her.

Pounding on the door, Tassie cried, "What ails you, Bella? Surely, you can tell me—I, who have stood by you through everything." When no reply came, the good woman sighed and complained, "But of course you do not regard what I say. Nobody regards me higher than that!" Here she snapped her finger for the benefit of the portraits on the wall.

On that note, the door opened a crack. Tassie could not see her cousin but she did hear her voice saying in a tone of subdued sorrow, "You would be very sorry if I let you in, Tassie. I am not fit company."

"What of that?" Tassie snapped. "You are never fit company. Why should today be different from any other day? Now let me in and I shall see if you have the fever.''

Isabella's reply was quiet but firm. "When I have collected myself and can meet a human creature without flying out at her, I shall see you." Thereupon, the door was shut.

Tassie wailed, "I know what has happened. You have failed to catch Ashton and we must all go to Cornwall." She burst into tears. The remainder of the day she spent in her chamber with a cool cloth on her head.

When Wild Goose appeared at her door, Isabella could not refuse her admittance, for the Iroquois promised to dance outside her door shaking a tortoiseshell rattle and beating a drum.

"It will take more than one of your turnips to cure me," Isabella declared, moving to the window to look out.

"You have sickness," Wild Goose informed her. She followed Isabella to the window and, thrusting her face forward so that she might inspect her, said, "Three things brings sickness: nature, witchcraft and desire of the soul."

Isabella nodded at this simple wisdom. "I would be obliged if you would kindly tell me how one cures desire of the soul."

"Fulfil the desire."

To Isabella's amazement, the Indian smiled. Her full lips revealed even white teeth. Isabella could not resist that hearty smile. She moved to the sofa and invited Wild Goose to sit beside her. "Tell me, please, is there among your people such a thing as divorce?"

Still smiling, Wild Goose replied, "We have very much divorce. My grandmother have fourteen husbands."

"Do you mean a lady may divorce her husband?"

"If she tire of him."

Isabella's eyes gleamed. "I hope she is not required to plead her case before Parliament, with witnesses and depositions and the like."

Wild Goose shook her head. "If wife wish divorce, she pile gear of husband in front of lodge."

"I should think the husband might take offence at such a summary dismissal."

"No, no. Is great honour for man to have many wives."

"What if a wife loves her husband and does not wish a divorce?"

The Indian laughed. "Wife always wish a divorce. Unmarried lady do as she please. Married lady is property of one man. Husband have power to trade wife, sell, beat or cut off ears. Better to divorce."

Isabella sighed. "Perhaps one day I shall teach myself to think so."

Wild Goose rose to leave. She was engaged to the Old Duke that afternoon, she said. He had expressly invited her to take tea with him and to bring with her any new cures she might have on her person, most especially those which might retard encroaching age. "I bring turkey wing, powdered root and wild sarsaparilla."

"Grandpapa will be delighted, I'm sure."

"While old man eat, I growl like bear."

"A stratagem guaranteed to work, as long as you first make him thoroughly uncomfortable. If you restore him to health too quickly, he will accuse you of quackery."

"This is great wisdom," Wild Goose said. At the door, she turned to add, "Do not forget, when desire granted, health returns. Is necessary to fulfil desire."

Isabella bowed her head. "There are some de-
sires," she said softly, "that can never be fulfilled."

THE VISIT from Wild Goose revived Isabella somewhat, so that she felt up to the task of deciding what
was to be done with Guy DuChateau. He must be
made to understand that his attachment would not do,
and the sooner she told him as much, the sooner he
might begin to recover from his disappointment.

Consequently, when the young man called the next
day at an hour much too early for civilized visiting, she
consented to have him shown to her sitting-room. As
the footman stood at the door, the Canadian strode
inside with all the vigour and confidence of youth, and
Isabella's heart went out to him. He was a beautiful
young gentleman; her acquaintance would have
thought her daft, romantical and perverse for refusing to let him love her. Such liaisons were rife among
her set. Perhaps, she said to herself, she *was* daft, romantical, perverse, but she was in love with her husband and could not help herself. Thus, she fixed Guy
with a serious look, placed her hands firmly on her
hips and scolded, "Dear boy, you must know that
henceforth there shall be no kissing and no displays of
any kind."

He smiled, not the least bit contritely.

Although she would have liked to smile, too, she did
not dare, for he could not be counted upon to take
such a demonstration in its proper spirit. Even if she
smiled in the most maternal, or, at any rate, sisterly
fashion, he would be sure to interpret her expression
in a manner better suited to his amorous inclinations.
Affixing a frown to her lips, she said, "Make no mistake, sir. I do not wish to flirt with you or encourage
you to flirt with me. From this moment forward, there

are to be no demonstrations of that kind, nothing that
is not consistent with the most disinterested friendship."

With a few long strides, he came to her, took her
hands and induced her to sit by him on the sofa. "I do
not wish to flirt," he said. "I wish to marry you. As
you are to be divorced, I see no reason why I may not
speak my heart openly."

She caught her breath, then, shaking her head, she
said, "You must marry a younger lady."

"Why?" he enquired. "The Prince favours ladies
who are far older than he is. Why may I not emulate
his example?"

"The Prince has one virtue: he sponsors the construction of acceptably aesthetic public works. Otherwise, he is silly and self-indulgent and I forbid you
to emulate him."

"Very well. I shall renounce him altogether. But I
do not intend to renounce you."

Isabella sighed, first because the boy would not be
persuaded to do what was in his best interests and
second because she was grateful for his amazing loyalty. She could not let him have his way, however. It
was wrong to allow Guy to love her when she was attached to someone else. Nobody knew better than she
the hollowness of loving without being loved in return.

Quietly, she said, "My dear boy, if you like, I shall
find a young lady for you to fall in love with. Nay, I
shall find an *old* lady for you to fall in love with, if you
prefer. But I pray you, do not present yourself to me
in the character of a husband. I have need of friends,
more than you know. I have the highest regard for
you, Guy, and I wish you to remain my friend through
life."

The power in her voice told him that she meant every syllable. His smile faded, though he made no attempt to argue. A momentary impulse seized him, so that he moved to kiss her, but she drew back. What he saw in her eyes, her divine green eyes, was absolute conviction. Nevertheless, he made one last effort, saying, "Mrs. Ashton. Isabella. I am in love with you."

She shook her head wearily. "It is absurd. You love me and I love another, who, in his turn, loves another. It all goes to prove that Cupid may as well dress himself up in medals and hats like Bonaparte, for all the destruction he wreaks. Whoever invented love ought to be hanged. Drawing and quartering, tarring and feathering are too good for him!"

"You are in love with someone else?" he repeated, for the rest of Isabella's speech had made scarcely any impression.

Rising from the sofa, she moved to the door. Throwing it open, she said gently, "You must go now."

He stood then and prepared to obey, stopping near her long enough to say with dignity, "As you are in love with another, I shall endeavour to accept my fate as well as I may."

His good-natured acquiescence caused her to smile. Earnestly, she clasped his hand and as she pushed him out the door, declared, "Thank you, dear boy. You are taking it wonderfully well. You may solace yourself with the knowledge that whereas the gentleman I love is lost to me, you shall always be my friend."

CHAPTER FIFTEEN

THE HOUSE in Upper Berkeley Street, Portman Square, which Ashton had taken for his Canadian charges, was a stately edifice in the centre of the fashionable district. From there, under Isabella's direction, they had lately been escorted to Gray's jewellers in Sackville Street, Twickenham in Middlesex, Twinings in the Strand and a hundred other destinations calculated to broaden the experience and views of all young ladies desiring an education in the world. In addition to sights, Celeste and Guy had been treated to countless tea parties, card parties and dancing parties, thanks to the vastness of Isabella's acquaintance. Now, as he sat in the large drawing-room of that elegant house, Ashton strove to absorb what he had lately been told: Isabella had lied about Mattingly, or, if not, then she was lying now. In either case, she was a liar.

He fixed his eyes on Celeste, who sat at a table with Chad, engrossed in watching him draw a map of one of Captain Cook's voyages. She had learned little geography and less natural history at school. Therefore, she was all the more fascinated by Chad Mattingly's expertise in these realms and watched without wavering as his slender hand drew cartographic images of land and sea. The sight of her so engrossed made him smile. Even if he were never free to declare himself, he acknowledged, seeing her would always make him smile.

This peaceful scene was interrupted by the entrance of Guy, who came to Ashton at once, pulled a chair near his and said, "Well, it is done. You ought to be perfectly satisfied in regard to Mrs. Ashton."

"Is she quite recovered from her illness?" Ashton enquired coolly.

"She is in excellent health. I know it all too well, for she sent me packing with singular energy."

Ashton glanced at him. "Packing? Are you certain?"

Guy laughed. "I believe I know when I have been sent packing. The lady will not have me. She forbids me to admire her from this day forward. There is not a shred of hope that she will change her mind."

Tapping his fingertips together, Ashton nodded in satisfaction. Despite her agitation of the day before, Bella had done as he had wished.

Guy stretched luxuriously and said, "Well, I daresay I shall not die of a broken heart. Mrs. Ashton has vowed to find me another lady to dance attendance on."

Ashton shook his head. How like Bella to seek a match for the very gentleman with whom she had just enjoyed a flirtation.

"Not that I shall soon forget Mrs. Ashton," Guy continued. "I am not so fickle as that. Still, forming a new acquaintance with a lady of beauty and charm will do much to take the sting out of my tragic disappointment. And given Isabella's own position, I expect she knew it would."

"What do you mean 'her own position'?"

"I mean that she too has been disappointed in love."

"Ridiculous. She has spent every moment in our company since our arrival. She has not had time to be disappointed in love."

"It appears she contrived to find the time, for she told me herself, this very day, that she is in love. I like to think that if not for this other gentleman, she might have loved me a little."

Ashton stood. He walked to where the portrait of a sneering nobleman hung. Sneering back at the fellow, he said with an edge, "Perhaps she was lying."

"Why should she lie?"

With an ironic half smile, he remarked, "I cannot begin to guess Isabella's motives for doing anything. Perhaps she said what she said to salve your pride."

"That is not a very flattering conjecture, but it could well be the truth. She said a great deal to ensure that we would always be on good terms, though not so cosy as I had hoped."

Although Guy had offered no objection to his suggestion, Ashton was still not entirely easy. Two years earlier Isabella had claimed to be in love. Now she claimed to have lied. Just minutes before, however, she had once again claimed to be in love. Was she telling the truth this time? What in blazes *was* the truth where Bella was concerned?

Looking up at the portrait, Ashton saw that the nobleman wore a smirk as well as a sneer. He turned his back on the disagreeable fellow and walked to where Celeste and Chad sat. Standing by the girl's chair, he gazed at her soft curls, admired her rosy arms and smiled at the attention she accorded the young Chad's pedantry. Because she was so rapt in the drawing, he forbore to interrupt. Instead, he approached Guy once more, saying, "I am convinced of it: Isabella would not have said she had broken her heart unless she meant to solace you.''

''She did not say her heart was broken. She said only that she was in love with a gentleman and that he is in love with somebody else.''

''And you believe her?''

''Why should I doubt her?''

Not vouchsafing more than a hurried goodbye, Ashton strode into the hall and instructed the servant to summon his horse and find his hat. He was done with debating and construing. The time had come to discover what, if anything, Isabella had said bore more than a nodding acquaintance with the truth. The time had come to learn whether this blackguard she claimed to love actually existed, and if so, who the deuce he was.

SHE WAS THOROUGHLY enjoying herself, weeping over a sentimental novel, when she heard a commotion in the house. Turning the key in her door, she crept to the head of the staircase and listened. From the voices below, she deduced that Ashton had called and that Tassie was endeavouring to explain that she had locked herself in the sitting-room and was denied to all visitors.

Quickly, she tiptoed back to the room, hid her novel under a cushion, located her sewing screen in a corner and arranged herself on the sofa so that she should be the picture of tranquil industry when Ashton entered.

That he would enter she did not doubt, for his voice had been low-pitched and stern, which she knew from of old meant he would not be stopped. Tassie's warnings, though sufficiently shrill and hysterical to discourage a Goliath, were doomed to go unheeded.

As Isabella had anticipated, she soon heard Ashton's step outside her door. At the sound of his three bold knocks, she called out sweetly, "Come."

He entered, pleased that he had not been compelled to break down the door, and stopped when he saw Isabella seated at her embroidery screen, busy at her work. As in the time of their domestic happiness, her slippers lay near the fire, one toe on top of the other. In her haste to arrange herself in an attitude of dignity, she had forgotten her shoes. Despite his angry determination to demand answers from her, the sight of her unshod feet caused him to smile.

"Oh, it is only you, Tony," she greeted him cheerfully. "How very convenient, for I have just received word from Grandpapa. We are all to attend the grand fête at Carlton House. You must go to Upper Berkeley Street at once and tell your cousins. Do not keep the news from them a moment longer."

He came inside, shutting the door behind him.

When it was clear that he meant to ignore her hint to be gone, she redoubled her concentration on her embroidery and said blithely, "I've been thinking of our late conversation, and it occurs to me that despite the inconvenient circumstances I was forced to confess, we may yet supply Mr. Doty with witnesses. I shall make Tassie say a word or two regarding the parade of lovers she has witnessed passing through these rooms, and if she refuses, I shall threaten her with Cornwall and shepherding. Three or four of the servants below have lived under this roof a hundred years at least and will be persuaded with guineas and lockets to say all that is necessary. I shall write them each a speech to recite to Mr. Doty. So you see, there will be no need to summon Mr. Combe or the others at the Museum for their testimony as to my faithlessness. We shall have witnesses in abundance. And so good day to you." When she jabbed her needle through a half-sewn bumblebee, the yellow thread came loose.

"Good day to you, too," he said. Instead of leaving, however, he took a chair facing her. He watched gravely as she attempted to rethread the needle. Her hands trembled.

"Gracious, you are still here," she said with a laugh.

"Yes. We have much to discuss, I believe."

She felt short of breath. "You will never guess who has been to see me. Mr. DuChateau, your cousin. He is a dear boy, is he not? But I forget myself. He is not a boy at all, as you have so cleverly reminded me. He is very much a young man, and such a young man! So handsome, so devoted, so young."

"In the courtyard of the Museum, you gave me to understand that Philip Mattingly was never more to you than a friend."

She paused with the thread in one hand and the needle in the other, then said lightly, "Yes, but as I have said, I shall not permit that nuisance to stand in the way of your divorce. You shall marry Celeste, and I shall marry her brother. Just minutes ago he begged me to give him my promise. And I could not refuse. He is such a dear boy."

Ashton sat back in his chair. His customary sternness hid his puzzlement. "Bella, are you now announcing that you are in love with Guy?"

She licked the thread in hopes it would go through the needle, but it would not. Giving it up for the moment, she replied airily, "Yes, I am excessively in love with him. Therefore, I hope we may hurry the divorce along, for I have come to find it slow and tedious. And Guy is so very impetuous, you know. He cannot wait to carry me off." Lifting her eyes to glimpse his face, she ventured, "I daresay you are equally impatient in regard to Miss DuChateau."

He sat perfectly still, not changing the expression on his lips, not so much as blinking. Once again, Isabella was lying. This time the symptoms were so obvious that he had all he could do to keep from laughing. She could not look him in the eye. Her voice quavered with false cheer. Her fingers could scarcely hold the needle.

Why? he asked himself. Why should she lie?

After giving him a quick glance, she grew somewhat alarmed at his thoughtful expression. To ease the tension, which felt as tight as a noose, she showed him a brilliant smile, resumed her efforts to thread the needle and observed, "But I need not urge you to hurry the divorce, I expect. You are as anxious as I am to remarry. Such a sweet wife Celeste will make you! Such a docile, obedient, sweet wife. And Guy is so much like her. What a docile, obedient, sweet husband he will make me."

Two years before, when she had spoken in this vein, he had listened, acquiesced and left her with a cool stateliness that he thought commensurate with his position as a wronged husband. The episode had transpired in that very house, nay, in that very room. Fate had now presented him with an opportunity to replay the same scene, and more than anything, he wished to replay it differently. If he did not, then he had learned nothing from his years of exile.

"You are lying, Bella," he said simply. Rising, he went to the sofa where she sat and, seating himself, took the needle and thread from her hands. When he had threaded the needle for her, he held it out and studied her astonished face.

She did not believe she had heard aright. She felt almost afraid to take the needle from him and just as afraid not to, for the expression on his face was powerfully intent. When at last she did take the needle, she noticed to her disgust that her fingers shook.

"I have just come from Guy," he said. "He told me you had sent him packing."

Caught, she dropped the threaded needle, rose and went to the fireplace, standing so that her back was to him.

"He told me that you refused to have him."

When she lowered her eyes, she saw her slippers warming by the hearth. She gasped and despaired. What was the use, she asked herself, of endeavouring to maintain one's dignity when one could not remember to put on one's shoes?

Calmly, he located the needle, safely inserted it into the embroidery cloth and came to her. "Guy also said that you were in love with another man."

She stifled a moan.

"He tells me that this unnamed gentleman is in love with another lady."

"If I had known that Mr. DuChateau was so little to be trusted, I should never had said a word to him!"

"Is there indeed such a gentleman, or is this another fabrication?"

Aware only of his dangerous nearness, she flung past him. In an offended voice, she said, "Are you impugning my veracity?" She stopped to glare at the half-finished picture she was embroidering. The bee snuggled up to a brilliant red poppy in the most irritating manner.

"You have lied about Mattingly. You have lied about Guy. And as far as I can tell, you had no more reason to lie in the one case than the other." He followed her and touched his hand to her arm.

She shrank from him. Then, summoning all her presence of mind, she said, "You are not so clever as you might think. It is true I lied when I said I meant to marry Guy, but I had a very good reason. By naming him, I was able to keep secret the true identity of my lover."

"I see. And why did you lie about Mattingly?"

"What does it matter?"

"I must know which of your lies is the truth."

She took a breath. Then, weary of evading his questions, she confessed, "I lied about Philip so that you would notice me. I thought that by telling you I loved him, you would do everything in your power to win me back. I was distracted at the time. When I lost William, I lost what little reason I possessed. I was mad enough to think that a twinge of jealousy would bring you back to me."

"So it was a trick."

She swallowed, then nodded.

He eyed her appreciatively. "You have explained your reasons for lying about Mattingly, but what of this new gentleman, the one you spoke of to Guy?"

A look of anguish crossed her face.

"Who is he?"

"I cannot tell you."

"He is married?"

"Yes."

"Tell me."

"You will never believe it."

"Still, you had better tell me."

Rebelliously, helplessly, she looked at him in silence. She made not a sound, but he saw the glistening in her eyes. The tears stung him. He had rarely seen her cry. With one swift movement, he came to her, folded his arms about her and caressed her so that she might sob on his chest. She seemed to flow into his embrace, as though she had carved a permanent place there. An instant later, she was clinging to him and alternately repressing her weeping and anointing his coat.

"Who is he?" Ashton whispered. "Tell me his name."

"I can't."

"Tell me. I will not leave this house until you tell me."

Heartsick, she cried, "King George!"

PART FOUR

Cricket

CHAPTER SIXTEEN

At that moment, the door opened. They sprang apart to see Tassie staring at them, her hands folded prayerfully, her mouth open, her eyes alight with triumph.

Some minutes earlier, she had gone to Isabella's bedchamber, and, surprised to find it empty, had crept to the sitting-room. For a time, she had listened at the door. Hearing nothing, she had tried the handle—slowly, so that she would not make a noise. The door had given way and opened a crack. She had peered in to discover her cousin in Ashton's arms. Unable to contain her rapture, she burst in on them.

"You must not mind me," Tassie gasped. "Indeed, nobody ever does." Backing from the room, grinning foolishly, she drew the door closed.

In the corridor, she gave a silent huzzah and performed a little dance. Isabella had done it, she exulted. She had vowed to win back Ashton and she had accomplished it. There would be no more talk of divorce, no more fear of scandal, no more nonsense about Cornwall and sheep, only kissing and embracing and rejoicing and keeping the carriage and the house in Town and the allowance and all the joys of life.

Ashton watched Bella, who, having recovered her composure, resumed her seat before the embroidery screen and endeavoured to sew. "I have stayed too late," he said, taking a few steps to the door. Her profile was fine and proud as she poked the needle through the bee.

She nodded, as though too absorbed in her work to do more than murmur a farewell.

"Good night," he said at the door.

"Goodbye," she replied.

As soon as she heard him go out, she put her hand to her throat and breathed again.

OUTSIDE, in the bracing night air, Ashton laughed.

King George! Again she had lied—and such a lie, such an outrageous, hilarious lie. It had told him more than the truth would have done: she was in love with him. He himself was the blackguard whose name he had demanded. That was why she had resisted his efforts to communicate with her about the divorce. That was why she was doing everything in her power to save face, because she was in love with him.

The sensation of her in his arms came back to him now, and he wished that he had kissed her. If Tassie had not come into the sitting-room at that moment, he would have kissed her. He was certain of it, for he had wanted very much to kiss her.

AS BELLA RECALLED Ashton's fleeting embrace, it came home to her that it bespoke not love but compassion. It would have been the most natural thing in the world for her to mistake it for love, given the multitude of erroneous conclusions she had formed these past weeks, but as no kiss had followed, no declaration, not even a murmur of feeling, she could not deceive herself that it represented anything more than a manly desire to protect the pathetic creature who could not remember her shoes or thread a needle without trembling or tell the simple truth. It was the same impulse, she supposed, which had led him to embrace her at St. Michael's. The recollection gave her a shudder. She could not bear to be an object of his charity. It was better to be hated than pitied.

"I will not be treated kindly!" Isabella proclaimed aloud. Returning the embroidery screen to its corner, she brushed her hands, as if a gesture of finality might succeed in dispelling the oppression of heart. She could not afford to pine, she told herself. An important matter required her attention: to wit, a plan for the future.

What was she to do with herself? It was a question she had been forced to ponder ever since Ashton had said he wished to marry Celeste. Recalling his words, she felt the heat rise to her cheeks. She knew she must not stay in London. She must quit her home in Hertford Street as soon as her agent could locate a secluded cottage not far from the sea. It was impossible to live where she would be reminded every day that instead of loving her, he loved the one creature in the world who was most unlike her.

Previously, she had given no serious thought to the future. Instead she had joked about exile in Cornwall and the aroma of sheep. After all, there was never going to be a divorce, was there? Once she had made Ashton realize that he was mad with love for her, he would give up the idea, horrified that he could ever have entertained the notion of separating himself for life from the only woman he had ever truly adored. It was the same wilful, irrational thinking she had employed when William lay sick with fever and she had refused to believe that he could die. Such thinking had done only harm. Now it behooved her to think sensibly.

Perhaps removing to Cornwall was not so absurd an idea as she had thought. Why had she found it so amusing? she asked herself. She had never set eyes on the place. For all she knew, it might be perfectly civilized. Like too many devotees of the Town, she had felt obliged to sneer at the rural regions. As it happened, she was no longer in a position to sneer.

Her imagination now leapt to Cornwall in earnest. She saw herself settling in a village of thatched cottages, populated by jolly countryfolk who carried their baskets to market and spoke in quaint, unintelligible accents. She thought of joining the ladies' book society, raising cucumbers and melons in a coldframe, and writing a romantic novel in which a beautiful but tragic heroine renounces the man she loves in order to do good works. These were charms which a week ago—nay, a day ago—would have raised satiric smiles. At the moment, however, they promised bliss. Anything was preferable to remaining where she must constantly be thrown in Ashton's way and subjected to his pity.

From this moment forward, she must avoid Ashton. No matter where he stood in a room, she must look to stand in the furthermost corner. If he addressed her, she must make a hasty answer and then put as much distance between them as possible. She must decline any invitation to ride with him in his carriage, and on no account must she be alone with him. These steps were crucial if she were to maintain her self-command in the trying days to come.

Straightening her shoulders, she made her way to her bedchamber. The hour was late, and she must endeavour to get a wink of sleep. She must not appear at

Carlton House with eyes red and swollen. It was one
thing to have all one's hopes dashed utterly to pieces,
quite another to appear before the Prince Regent
looking like an owl.

EARLY THE NEXT MORNING, Tassie repaired to an es-
critoire to write a letter to the Old Duke:

> My Lord Duke,
> It is my very great pleasure to tell you that there
> is to be no divorce. Our dear Isabella has suc-
> ceeded. I wished to give you the earliest possible
> intelligence of the glad tidings, for I am certain
> you will rejoice, as we all must.
> I am, your most devoted servant,
>   Tatiana Terwilliger

Contrary to Tassie's conjecture, the Old Duke did
not rejoice. The news debilitated him utterly. It would
require more herbal remedies than even Princess Wild
Goose could minister before he would recover from his
connection with a nobody. Happily, Wild Goose
thought to introduce her patient to a game of dice in
which the stakes were earrings, collars and locks of
hair. The distraction proved salubrious, and the duke
did not notice that the Iroquois fleeced him without
mercy.

Relieved though he must have been that no divorce
would now transpire to tarnish the Wortwell name, he
was determined to point out to Isabella all the misery
and shame in store for her as the life's companion of
a mere Ashton. Therefore, throughout the carriage
ride to Carlton House, he regaled her with an ac-
counting of her husband's many faults. No quality of

Ashton's—his fashions, figure, face, fortune or family—escaped the duke's sharp-tongued censure.

Ordinarily, Isabella would have raised an objection to this manner of being entertained. On this occasion, however, she let her grandfather's ill-natured speech flow, hoping that he might accidentally hit upon some observation that would reconcile her to what must be. Before that event, however, they arrived in the vicinity of Carlton House. It was nine o'clock, and the string of waiting carriages extended as far as Bond Street. A crowd had gathered to ogle the guests in their equipages and to call out hoots and howls. As the duke's carriage inched forward, Isabella saw Ashton's. Celeste appeared at the window, waving to her and calling her name. Anxious to avoid Ashton, Isabella pretended not to see. As she turned away, she caught a glimpse of Celeste's astonished face. She felt remorseful at having inadvertently affronted the poor girl, but she knew not what else to do.

When at last the carriage reached Carlton House, Isabella, in an effort to avoid meeting Ashton, descended quickly and hurried onto the torch-lit portico, pulling her grandfather after her. Nevertheless, the two parties did meet on the portico. After the young Canadians were introduced to the Old Duke, who condescended to kiss the young lady's hand, Celeste greeted Isabella warmly and said, "Did you not see us drive up? I called to you."

Conscious of Ashton's presence, Isabella replied that her head was entirely filled with delighted anticipation of the delightful pleasures in store for them all that evening.

Eagerly, Celeste entered into this excess of delight, adding, "I should have looked forward with even greater anticipation had Mr. Mattingly been invited, too. Indeed, when he told me that he was not to come, I could scarcely credit it.''

Composing herself, Isabella replied, ''I understand that the invitations were given out somewhat haphazardly. Husbands have been forced to attend without their wives in some cases. A number of invitations were sent to girls who are not yet out; others were sent to men who are no longer living. Happily, you and your brother were not overlooked.''

''I am glad that Wild Goose consented to sit with Mr. Mattingly tonight,'' Celeste said. ''I am certain he would be desolate otherwise.''

At the first opportunity, Isabella glanced at Ashton, who returned her gaze. The warmth of his expression shook her. Impulsively, she seized Guy's arm and hurried him towards the entrance hall lined with marble columns. As they walked, she sent up a prayer that she might survive the evening with tolerable dignity. That she should look to preserve her dignity at all was unprecedented, and she could not help but think to what depths love had lately made her sink.

Isabella's hurrying off amazed Celeste. Anxiously, she asked Ashton if he thought she had done something to offend Mrs. Ashton.

From the instant he had set eyes on Bella, from the second he had beheld her sumptuous gown of lush green satin and her soft expanse of back, Ashton foresaw a difficult evening ahead. It would take a will of iron to keep his eyes off her. He guessed that her object was to avoid him, and he found that fact amusing, because he had spent the previous hours wondering how he might contrive to be alone with her among two thousand guests at Carlton House.

A moment with Isabella was all he needed to understand his heart fully. So far, he knew only that she

attracted him, a fact which took him somewhat by
surprise. After all, they had spent two years apart;
time ought to have done its work. Yet now he desired
her as much as he had on the day he had proposed
marriage to her. He was forced to acknowledge that
thirty, fifty, *seventy* years in Canada would not serve
to diminish that desire.

Celeste brought him back to the present by repeat-
ing her expressions of alarm regarding Isabella. "She
means to cut me," she mourned. "I have made some
hideous *faux pas,* for which she cannot forgive me."

"You have not offended Bella," he assured her.
"You must not reproach yourself."

She sighed and would have argued further, but he
put a gentle finger to her lips and led her to the entrance hall, which was so spacious and grand as to
cause the girl to forget Isabella altogether and gasp in
awe. With a crowd of other guests attired in their best
satin and diamonds, they were conducted on a tour of
rooms full of wonders; rooms furnished with claw-
footed gilt chairs and tables; rooms painted, papered,
carpeted, carved, curtained and ornamented in blues,
roses and golds; rooms bathed in light that echoed
their gorgeous hues; rooms lit by crystal-and-gold
chandeliers hung from ceilings so high that Celeste was
forced to throw back her head to admire them.

The guests crowded into the assembly rooms, hoping to catch a glimpse of the Regent or his illustrious
guest, King Louis of France. The Old Duke led the
way through the crush towards the ballroom, which
was too crowded for dancing. In the distance, the
Prince Regent appeared, dressed in a rich scarlet uni-
form with a star on his chest and a sabre at his waist.
Applause greeted his entrance. Graciously, he welcomed his guests, apologized for the renovations of

the house which were still in progress, and hoped they would all go and see his latest acquisition, a painting by the Dutchman Rembrandt, which had cost five thousand guineas.

Celeste swallowed hard, overcome by the sight of the Regent, but her attention was soon summoned by several gentlemen overcome by the sight of her. In the absence of Wild Goose, Guy steadied her with a strong hand and prevented the beaux from flattering his sister out of countenance. The duke went off in search of less disgraceful companions. Isabella and Ashton were left alone.

Both of them soon became aware of the lack of air in the room. Just as Ashton addressed an inconsequential remark to her, Isabella bowed her head, murmured an excuse and moved quickly away. She eased herself between two large, corseted and feathered matrons and pushed through the crowd until she had placed herself well out of danger. With a breath of relief, she looked about her.

Distraction soon presented itself in the person of Mr. Sheridan, who related a witty anecdote to a small collection of listeners. As she heard his monologue, Isabella demonstrated a fortitude which pleased her, for she did not glance in Ashton's direction above half a dozen times.

When Guy and Celeste looked round, they found Ashton standing quite alone. They enquired after Isabella and were informed that she might be found on the other side of the room.

While Guy went in search of her, Celeste frowned and declared to Ashton, "I am certain now that I have offended her. Indeed, I had a hint of it at the Museum. Her leaving so suddenly betokened some offence, I believe. Illness was merely an excuse. I have insulted her, and now she looks to avoid me. She hates the very sight of me." In the course of this worried speech, her voice quavered until, at the last words, she actually shed two shining tears.

To comfort her, Ashton patted her hand and said, "You are not at fault, my dear."

"But she has never before behaved with such aloofness. I don't know what else to make of it. Clearly, she thinks I have done something dreadful."

"If Bella appears aloof, I expect the fault is mine."

With brimming eyes, Celeste regarded him. He felt the force of her guileless, trustful look.

"Do you mean to say that it is *you* who has offended her?"

Smiling a little, he said, "I do not believe I have offended her precisely, but I do believe that I, and not you, am the cause of her odd behaviour."

Abruptly, Celeste put her hands to her cheeks and cried, "Oh, this cannot be. There is nothing so distressing to me as seeing the people I am most fond of at odds with each other."

"My dear, Bella and I are always at odds with each other. No one would recognize us if we were otherwise."

She could not return his quizzing smile. Solemnly, she pleaded, "You must make it up with her. I cannot abide a quarrel. You must make it up at once." And, not pausing to expostulate further, she led him by the hand through the crush.

THE INSTANT Guy caught sight of Isabella, she beckoned to him and whispered that she had found the perfect female on whom he might bestow his adoration, which had been at liberty several days and nights and must now find some useful occupation. A lady of a certain age, she was the widow of an admiral, the widow of a baronet and, most recently, the widow of a marquess. "To have outlived three husbands of such high position," Isabella said, "she must be very accomplished."

Upon introduction to Lady Suppel, Guy was captivated, for not only was she attractive and charming, but she looked him up and down in a manner which rendered him most pleasantly warm about the collar. Although the lady had been enthralled by Mr. Sheridan's wit, it was the work of a moment to transfer her brilliant smile to the young Canadian. Isabella noted that while her lips were silent, her eyes spoke fulsomely; while her hands and arms were sheathed in the silkiest of white gloves, her pink feet were nearly bare in the flimsiest of sandals; while her bodice dipped low, her breasts rose high. Guy asked if he might be permitted to kiss the hand of his charming new acquaintance. Huskily, she replied that she did not think she could ever deny a request made by such a devilishly handsome gentleman. On that, he threw Isabella a look of gratitude.

Isabella was congratulating herself on having thoroughly mended the young gentleman's broken heart when she felt an urgent tug on her arm. Turning, she saw Celeste and, behind her, Ashton. The girl was uncharacteristically insistent. "You must make it up!" she cried. "If you and Ashton are not on good terms, I do not know what is to become of us all." Impetuously, she seized Isabella's hand, placed it in Ashton's, and with one imploring look, asked her brother to take her outside for a breath of air. With Celeste on one arm and Lady Suppel on the other, Guy made his way to the tent.

As soon as Isabella made a vow not to meet Ashton's eyes, she broke it. His soft expression confused her. She was very conscious that he held her hand, and she cautioned herself to be on her guard.

"Celeste has taken it into her head that we have quarrelled," he said.

His steadfast look made her colour. She felt like a foolish girl just out of the schoolroom. Even when she had in fact been a foolish girl just out of the schoolroom, she had felt more at ease.

"It is all my fault," Isabella declared, trying to sound careless. "I meant to give you and Celeste every opportunity of being private together. Instead, I gave her the impression that I was vexed with her."

"I have told her that I am the one you wish to avoid, but she is determined that everyone she knows get on well with one another. She will not allow any of us to quarrel, much as we might like to."

She tried not to look at the hand which held hers.

"We might as well accept our fate with a good grace," he said, smiling. "She will keep throwing us in each other's way until we do."

Isabella was wondering how she would endure such a fate, when she saw him look about the room. Suddenly he caught her with his eyes. "What do you say to viewing the Rembrandt?" he asked.

Lightly, she replied, "I detest Rembrandt. Really, he is quite the amateur."

His grip on her hand prevented her leaving his side. With uncommon intensity, he said, "If we do not seize our opportunity now, Bella, we may never have another."

She wondered if the meaning she heard was the meaning he intended to convey. "I declare, Tony," she said laughing carelessly, "if what you wish to see is prosaic faces squinting in half-light, you may visit the House of Lords. You need not put yourself to the trouble of seeking out Rembrandt.''

He smiled. ''My dearest wife, if the nation has spent five thousand guineas it can ill afford solely in order to purchase the painting, it is our patriotic duty to see it.'' So saying, he firmly tucked her hand in his arm and led her from the room.

CHAPTER SEVENTEEN

SHE WAS ENTRANCED by *The Shipbuilder and His Wife*. However, Ashton found his thoughts wandering from the long-married pair in the painting. He wished to find a corner conducive to a tête-à-tête, and the task was difficult, owing to the omnipresence of gawking guests and solicitous servants. At last, by proposing that they tour the rooms, he persuaded her to tear her eyes from the masterpiece.

After some time spent wandering, he contrived to attain the Blue Velvet Room, which was quite empty. It was adorned in a sleepy blue-grey from its soft carpet to its tall painted ceiling. To view the depictions on the ceiling, they were required to sit on one of the blue velvet settees. From that vantage point, they took in the three-tiered gilt chandeliers which gave off a sparkling blue light.

All the while she admired the ceiling, Isabella told herself that she had to leave before it was too late. If she did not escape Ashton's presence that very minute, she would not be answerable for the event.

Ashton was too preoccupied with studying the green of her eyes to admire the azure glow which surrounded them.

Feeling his gaze on her, Isabella said brightly, "I wish Celeste were more like other girls and took pleasure in the enmity of others. I suspect the child

does not know what malice is. It is highly unnatural.''
She then rose as a prelude to exiting.

Immediately, he rose, too. In a single motion, he put
his hand round her waist and moved near.

She swallowed.

His face moved closer, until it was a breath away.

''No,'' she whispered.

In reply, he lightly brushed her lips with his. Then,
remembering every iota of their former intimacy, he
held her to him and kissed her hungrily.

Isabella yielded, even while she resisted. Instinc-
tively, she moved her hands along his shoulders until
they met behind his neck. She concluded that resis-
tance was futile and that she was quite doomed. There
was nothing left to do but give herself up completely,
and she would have pressed herself to him with an
aching, but a noise summoned their attention. They
looked up to see the Prince Regent, clearing his throat
behind his hand, and the Old Duke by his side, scowling.

At once, Isabella and Ashton parted and dutifully
performed all signs of respect to His Royal Highness.
Smiling, he complimented them on their billing and
cooing and invited them to please continue. Not for
the world would he interrupt his guests enjoying the
pastime which all the world knew best suited his own
taste and talent.

''I beg Your Highness's pardon,'' said Ashton,
''and I ask your indulgence.''

''Indulgence!'' declared the Prince. ''Yes, there is
nothing I am so ready to grant myself and anyone else
as indulgence. Come,'' he said to the Old Duke, ''let
us leave these turtle-doves so that they may become
better acquainted.''

The Old Duke did not stir. "They are already acquainted, I fear," he remarked stonily.

"I like the two of them prodigiously," the Prince declared. "They conduct themselves in the Blue Velvet Room as is right and proper, if only one dared."

"They conduct themselves disgracefully," the duke snorted.

Planting an elbow in the Old Duke's aged rib, the Prince whispered, "How can you talk in such a prudish style? Have you no compassion for lovers?"

"They are not lovers. They are married."

The benign expression the Regent wore faded. It was replaced by a grimace, as though he had just tasted vinegar when he thought to have had wine. He raised his glass to his eye, looked the lady and gentleman over from top to toe, and asked, "Is it true? You are married—to each other?"

"It is true, Your Highness," Ashton confessed with a slight smile.

The Regent stepped back, lest some dread contagion spread to his royal person.

To soothe his evident shock, Isabella said hastily, "I assure Your Highness, we are scarcely married at all. Because Mr. Ashton has just returned after two years' residence in Canada, we are more like strangers than man and wife."

Curious to witness in the flesh a married couple who liked each other well enough to permit their lips to touch, the Prince gaped at them. First he studied Ashton, who seemed a fine figure of a gentleman and not the least mad. Next, his gaze shifted to Isabella who also appeared to be in complete possession of her faculties. Then, addressing the Old Duke, the Prince said, "What is one to make of these two?"

"One can only be shocked, shocked and aggrieved."

"Oh, piffle!" the Regent scoffed. "Surely you have taken advantage of an opportunity now and again to kiss a handsome female."

"Of course, Your Highness, but never my own wife!"

The Prince was compelled to allow that the Old Duke spoke sensibly, for he himself had never voluntarily kissed his own wife and he never intended to. At the same time, as a man whose family had endeavoured to separate him from the lady he did love so that he might marry one he despised, he thought it behooved him to champion the charming lovers who stood before him. He could not find it in his heart to hold their marital condition against them. Consequently, he said, "Clearly you disapprove, Wortwell, but you must not do so any longer. It pleases me to bestow my blessing on this charming couple. You will oblige me by doing likewise."

The Old Duke went white beneath his rouge. Because he was in the Prince's confidence, he ventured to express a small objection, saying deferentially, "Perhaps I ought to mention, Your Highness, that Ashton here has no blood."

"Bother his blood!" he declared. "The man has juice! If Mrs. Ashton requires nothing more, I do not see that we have anything to say to it."

The duke reddened and clapped his mouth shut.

"It will not do," remarked the Regent as he observed the effect of his words on the duke. "You look as though you have sucked lemons. Come, now. I insist that you smile."

Hearing the royal command, the Old Duke showed his teeth.

"Excellent. Now you must shake hands with Ashton."

Ashton could not forbear smiling as the Old Duke was compelled to shake his hand.

"While I engage this beauteous lady in conversation," said the Prince, "I shall leave you excellent gentlemen to negotiate a treaty of peace between you."

On that, he levelled an appreciative look at Isabella. Although she was somewhat younger than what he generally admired in the female sex, she was attired in a gown which clung most delectably. Moreover, he recollected that he had heard her ivory back spoken of with the highest praise. The more he looked at her, the more he felt the impulse to view her back.

"Would you care to see my new painting?" he asked her graciously. "It is a great masterpiece and cost five thousand guineas."

Out of reverence for his position, Isabella refrained from saying that she had lately come from admiring *The Shipbuilder and His Wife.* She nodded and put her hand on the Prince's proffered arm. As he led her from the Blue Velvet Room, Isabella was surprised to find that he continually glanced behind her.

He was still craning his neck in that manner when they reached the Rembrandt, so that Isabella could not help asking at last, "Have I torn my hem, Your Highness? Perhaps I have stained my gown?"

The Prince declared he would be prodigiously obliged if she would stand still for a bit and look at the dratted painting, which, in case he had not mentioned it before, cost five thousand guineas. Meanwhile, he would take the opportunity to stand behind her and observe her as she observed the masterpiece.

Odd as the request was, Isabella complied, though she strongly suspected that the Prince might have been seized with the same malady of mind which afflicted his poor father. For the next several minutes, she fixed her eyes on the married couple before her while the Prince fixed his eyes on her back.

THE OLD DUKE and Ashton took the measure of each other in silence.

At last, the duke said, "My Regent has commanded me to shake your hand, and I obey. I can never approve your marriage to my granddaughter, but a Wortwell knows what is owed to King and Country."

"I scarcely know how to be grateful for such amiable complaisance," Ashton said with an ironic smile, "for I am wholly unused to it."

The duke, who was impervious to irony, pointed at him with his carved ebony walking stick, saying, "I suppose I must be reconciled, for if there is to be no divorce, then I had better get used to having you underfoot."

Ashton raised his brows. "I beg your pardon. What is it you said in regard to divorce?"

Irritably, the Old Duke threw up his tails behind him and lowered himself onto the blue settee. Inhaling the scent of his linen, he said, "I know everything regarding your plan to divorce Bella, and it is well you have come to your senses about it. My intention has always been to prevent such an action; it has been Bella's intention, as well. Now that we have achieved our end, I am prepared to do what must be done, despite my abhorrence. I therefore," and here he shuddered before saying, "welcome you to the family. You will, I trust, overlook the belatedness of the welcome."

As Ashton drew near, his expression began to take on some of its characteristic sternness. "What gives you the notion that I have thought better of the divorce?"

"You need not pretend, sir. As I have said, I know everything."

"I did not know you were in Bella's confidence."

"My granddaughter knows who it is she can trust."

"You say that Bella has endeavoured to prevent the divorce, but that is highly unlikely, I think. She has never said a word in opposition. Indeed, she has shown herself unnaturally complaisant on the subject."

"Well, of course she has been complaisant. A Wortwell is not a fool. I daresay if she had openly opposed the divorce, you would never have given up the idea, would you? It requires a certain subtlety to persuade some creatures to do as they ought."

"You imply that Bella has been scheming." He would have added that the charge was nothing short of vicious, but he was silenced by the recollection of another scheme, one to which Bella had recently confessed.

"I imply only that she has conducted herself properly in regard to her family. As she has done exactly right, I am prepared to acknowledge you as her husband. I hope you are content now, for you have won your point."

What Ashton felt at the moment bore no resemblance to contentment. Angrily, he retorted, "If what you say is true, it is not *I* who have won my point but Bella who has won hers."

Smoothing the folds of lace at his wrists, the Old Duke sniffed, "Whoever has won the point, it has certainly not been myself. Nevertheless, I withdraw my opposition to this marriage, not only because my Regent says that I must, but also because I know, as Bella knows, that a divorce among the Wortwells cannot be permitted.''

As Ashton absorbed all the implications of the duke's words, the events of the past months flashed through his mind. He began to see Isabella's conduct in a new light. Her invitation to the party at Hertford Street, her kindness to Celeste, her flirtation with Guy, her insistence that they all be cosy, her behaving as though she were in love with him—these actions struck him now as premeditated steps in a campaign to woo him. Only by winning him back could she hope to prevent what must end her life in London Society and damage the Wortwell name. Only by winning him back could she prevent the divorce.

It struck him that he had been singularly naïve. In Canada, he had trapped wily beaver, landed outsize fish, fought ravenous wolves and overcome cold and hunger, but a lone antagonist—one whose sole weapons were her emerald eyes, her bare back and her outrageous unpredictability—had nearly defeated him. If he had not felt such acute, such passionate anger, he would have laughed. Of all people, he ought to have known better.

The Old Duke rose, leaning heavily on his cane. Primly, he adjusted his person so that he presented the picture of a perfectly arranged gentleman of the ton. He was on the point of taking his leave when Ashton detained him.

''I have been thinking how to disabuse you of your misapprehension,'' he said. ''There is no use in disguising the truth. My only recourse, I fear, is to tell it plainly. I had no intention of reversing my position as regards the divorce. I never meant to do anything but dissolve my marriage, and, as Bella has kindly offered to provide me with all the grounds the law requires, I mean to pursue the action with all due haste."

The duke stared. He had already accommodated himself to one disagreeable fact that evening. He did not intend to adjust his thinking again. Shaking his head obstinately, he stated, "You say that merely to vex me. You are not serious."

Ashton smiled. "Soon you will know precisely how serious I am."

Appalled, the Old Duke cried, "But you kissed her. I saw you, there on the settee. Why should you kiss her if you did not mean to keep her as your wife?"

Ashton walked towards the door.

"I smoke it!" the Old Duke cried, stopping him. He directed an elegantly gloved finger at Ashton's chest and said, "You wish to have your revenge! You believe she betrayed you, and now you mean to jilt her. That is the reason, is it not?"

With a half smile, Ashton said, "Revenge will do very well for a reason," and strode from the room.

WHILE THE PRINCE and his party repaired to the Gothic Dining Room, the others went to supper in the garden, where a tent had been erected and ornamented with flowers and illuminated glass. The tables gleamed with service of gold and silver. Like the setting, the feast was entirely splendid. It consisted of hot roasts and soups, cold meats, an abundance of fruits and, to quench the thirst, superb wines and iced champagne. Had Isabella noticed any part of the sumptuous display, she would have relished its excess. As it was, she saw nothing. While the guests chewed, roared and revelled on all sides, she moved a morsel of beef about her plate and replayed in her mind the scene in the Blue Velvet Room.

He had kissed her. It might mean nothing, or it might mean everything; she could not be certain. After her earlier mistakes, she dared not risk leaping to any conclusion. But the indisputable fact remained: he had kissed her.

She strove to rein in her imagination, telling herself that he might have kissed her merely out of curiosity, a wish to see to what extent their long separation had affected their former attraction. Or he might have kissed her simply because the opportunity was there. But another voice whispered that he would not have kissed her unless he desired her. It was a small step, she had always believed, from the expression of desire to an admission of love.

This charming reverie came to an abrupt end when Isabella felt a voice in her ear. Her dinner companion, a gentleman who greatly resembled a hawk, demanded her attention. She was informed in a whisper that the Prince had appeared and was bowing to her from the head of the vast table.

Isabella glanced up to see the Prince wave to her and nod. He had evidently left the Gothic Dining Room, where he had dined with the King of France and the noblest lights of the kingdom, to do the pretty to his lesser guests in the tent. With an effort, he heaved his person to a standing position. He raised his glass of champagne and, fixing Isabella with a moist look, announced, "I hereby make a proclamation, to wit, that any and all wives be permitted to kiss their husbands in both the public and private rooms of Carlton House—unless, of course, she be *my* wife." He called on the Old Duke, who accompanied him, to join him in drinking, and when he and everybody else

had drunk, applauded, and replied with toasts of their
own, he sank into a chair and delicately ate a straw-
berry.

Wondering how Ashton might be bearing up under
this quizzing, Isabella looked his way. He was seated
at a distance with Celeste and Guy and appeared not
to have heard a word of the foregoing, so engrossed
was he in holding a tart to Celeste's lips and coaxing
her to eat.

Isabella stared. She had seen Ashton stern, cross,
soft, harsh, ardent and ironic. Not until now had she
seen him playful. He teased Celeste, laughed with uncharacteristic gaiety and, when he induced her to take
a bite, offered another for her delectation. Isabella's
cheeks grew warm as she acknowledged a pang of
envy.

At the start of the evening, she had wished only that
he might avoid her as much as she intended to avoid
him. Now, it appeared, her wish had been granted, for
not once, through the whole of the meal, did he so
much as glance her way. When the supper was done
and the ladies rose to withdraw, he still kept his eyes
averted. Isabella wondered whether he regretted the
kiss in the Blue Velvet Room, or, worse, whether she
had only imagined it.

Weary with eating, drinking and revelry, Isabella
murmured a word to the hawkish gentleman by her
side and quickly left the tent. There, under the stars
and torchlights, she inhaled and tried to make sense of
the evening's events.

Before long, Celeste found her. "Oh, Mrs. Ashton,
I beg the favour of your assistance. I do not know
what I shall do."

Isabella could not resist smiling at the girl. "Whose
quarrel do you wish to patch this time?"

Celeste blushed prettily. "I know of no quarrel, I am thankful to say. Mr. Ashton assures me that you and he are now on the same terms as formerly, and I am gratified. But what I have to ask you has to do with a matter which is far more difficult than any quarrel."

Isabella asked what this dire matter could possibly be.

"Cricket," the girl said.

Isabella repressed a laugh. "Indeed, fond as I am of the sport, I must allow it is alarming. How may I be of assistance?"

"While we were at table, a bet was got up among several gentlemen who wish to have a ladies' match at Ball's Pond. I am to be one of the players." Here she frowned as though she appreciated for the first time the enormity of what she had done in agreeing to such a plan.

"You need not feel any trepidation. I suppose you have been invited to play a match in which the teams comprise both gentlemen and ladies. Such matches are generally quite gentle, my dear. You need not even wield a bat, for ladies are, as a rule, well supplied with broom handles."

"Oh, no, they vow the match is to consist only of ladies, and they talk of its being dreadfully rough. You are fond of the sport, Mr. Mattingly tells me, and highly knowledgeable. If you do not help me, I shall make myself a laughing-stock."

"What would you like me to do?"

"You can tell me what cricket is, for I have no idea."

"Nobody does, I assure you."

"If you could tell me the rules, I should at least not be entirely ignorant."

"If anyone knew what the rules were, Miss Du-Chateau, I should not hesitate to tell you, but they defy comprehension."

"Then you will not help me."

She looked so forlorn at this conclusion that Isabella was forced to put aside all joking. Impulsively, she patted the girl's hand and said, "But of course I shall help you."

At this juncture, the gentlemen emerged from the tent.

Seeing Ashton, Celeste ran to him and led him to where Isabella stood. Instead of looking at her, he seemed to look past her.

"We are in luck!" Celeste declared. "Mrs. Ashton has been prevailed upon to teach me cricket, so that I shall not put everyone to the blush with my wretched skill." On this, she smiled happily at each of them in turn.

Isabella caught the barest glimpse of Ashton's sternness; then she, too, looked away. The softness he had shown in the Blue Velvet Room was gone.

"Certainly Mrs. Ashton must teach you cricket," he said with an edge to his tone. "If anyone can make head or tail of its intricacies, it is she. I daresay she understands them so well that she may even show you how to cheat."

Summer Reading At Its Best

In July, Harlequin and Silhouette bring readers the Big Summer Read Program. Heat up your summer with these four exciting new novels by top Harlequin and Silhouette authors.

SOMEWHERE IN TIME by Barbara Bretton
YESTERDAY COMES TOMORROW by Rebecca Flanders
A DAY IN APRIL by Mary Lynn Baxter
LOVE CHILD by Patricia Coughlin

From time travel to fame and fortune, this program offers something for everyone.

Available at your favorite retail outlet.

FREE GIFT OFFER

With Free Gift Promotion proofs-of-purchase from Harlequin or Silhouette, you can receive this beautiful jewelry collection. Each item is perfect by itself, or collect all three for a complete jewelry ensemble.

For a classic look that is always in style, this beautiful gold tone jewelry will complement any outfit. Items include:

Gold tone clip earrings (approx. retail value $9.95), a 7½" gold tone bracelet (approx. retail value $15.95) and a 18" gold tone necklace (approx. retail value $29.95).

FREE GIFT OFFER TERMS

To receive your free gift, complete the certificate according to directions. Be certain to enclose the required number of Free Gift proofs-of-purchase, which are found on the last page of every specially marked Free Gift Harlequin or Silhouette romance novel. Requests must be received no later than July 31, 1992. Items depicted are for illustrative purposes only and may not be exactly as shown. Please allow 6 to 8 weeks for receipt of order. Offer good while quantities of gifts last. In the event an ordered gift is no longer available, you will receive a free, previously unpublished Harlequin or Silhouette book for every proof-of-purchase you have submitted with your request, plus a refund of the postage-and-handling charge you have included. Offer good in the U.S. and Canada only.

MILLIONAIRE! *Sweepstakes!*

As an added value every time you send in a completed certificate with the correct number of proofs-of-purchase, your name will automatically be entered in our Million Dollar Sweepstakes. The more completed offer certificates you send in, the more often your name will be entered in our sweepstakes and the better your chances of winning.

PROI

CHAPTER EIGHTEEN

THE CARRIAGE JOUNCED its inmates sufficiently to lull the Old Duke into a doze and to induce Isabella to lose herself in thought. Ashton's conduct during the previous hours mystified her as much as cricket mystified Celeste. Early in the evening, he had gazed at her warmly, spoken with intensity and then done precisely what she had given over all hope of his ever doing: he had kissed her. When next she had stood near him, he was scarcely the same man; he had grown cold, ironic and stern. What could have brought about such a reversal?

Perhaps, she thought, it was the kiss. Perhaps it had disappointed him. Sorely out of practice these two years, she had not been certain what to do with her lips while his pressed them. She had meant to return the kiss, but she had not made her intention sufficiently clear to him.

The very first time he had kissed her she had been nearly as innocent as Celeste, if such a thing were possible. Naturally, her kisses had been those of an innocent. That is to say, she had held her lips pursed, as though preparing to whistle, until he had quite finished. After they were married, however, there had come substantial improvement.

Given her age, Isabella thought, her skill ought to have continued to improve. Instead, owing to long disuse, it had evidently declined. She sank to think that she had probably greeted his kiss the way a turbot greets the aspic in which it is served. It was no wonder he had felt let down.

Although the likelihood of her ever having the opportunity to redeem herself was infinitesimal, wisdom dictated that she prepare for such an eventuality, especially as she had twice been surprised by kisses in recent days and wished to perform creditably if the need arose at some future date. Accordingly, she wet her lips, first the bottom then the top, then pressed them forward in what seemed to her an attitude of readiness. For a time, she moved them in the manner of the turbot who had lately occupied her thoughts. Satisfied that her lips were sufficiently limber to accomplish any effort they might be called upon to exert, she sought a means of testing her skill.

To that end, she removed a glove and placed the back of her bare hand a quarter inch from her lips. Then she kissed it. Her first trial proved too smackingly loud; her second, too limp; her third, too athletic. She would have combined the best features of each had she not looked up to see her grandfather staring at her in heavy-lidded horror.

Laughing, Isabella explained, "I am practising my kisses, Grandpapa. Kissing is an art, like playing the pianoforte. One must keep it up or lose the facility."

He shifted his creaking bones and remarked, "You need not go to the bother, my dear. Mr. Anthony Ashton will not kiss you again."

She coloured. "That is for me to decide, Grandpapa."

"You might as well know it all. The kiss he gave you tonight was by way of revenge. His intention was only to mortify you. He told me so himself."

"Revenge?"

Petulantly, he said, "Mr. Anthony Ashton is without doubt the most obstinate, contrary, irrational fellow I have ever had the misfortune to be connected to. But what can one expect from a man who has no blood? Exactly what one has received, I suppose—revenge. The wronged husband turns the tables and all that!"

Shocked, she replied, "Did he tell you he was a wronged husband?"

"Of course not. Tassie told me he believed he was. Do you think I should have learnt anything of the Mattingly business otherwise? You certainly did not have the courtesy to confide in me. Happily, Tassie knows what is owed to the head of a family, even one that is not her own."

"I have never known Tony to be vengeful."

The Old Duke snarled, "I tell you, he is worse than vengeful. He is an ungrateful puppy. How does he thank me for procuring invitations to Carlton House for those foreigners of his? By gloating over this divorce. It is insupportable."

Under the cover of the semidarkness, Isabella brushed something from her cheek.

"Only want of blood can explain such ingratitude in a man. A man with no blood will always have recourse to spite."

"Do not say any more, please."

"The upshot is that your plan must be pronounced a failure. I tell you, the entire affair will end in ruining my complexion."

"What plan do you mean?"

"Why, the plan to get him to give up the divorce. What other plan is there?"

Appalled, Isabella asked, "How did you hear of such a plan?"

"Tassie told me. I confess, I heard of it with relief, for I feared you actually intended to allow such a calamity to befall the family."

"How could she have told you? It was to be a secret."

"What is the good of a secret if it is not told, especially to your grandpapa, my dear?"

Isabella despaired.

"Some days ago, I received the intelligence from Tassie that your plan had succeeded, that Ashton had regained his wits and was ready to give up the divorce. Yet, when I congratulated him, he denied having any such intention. The fellow does not know his own interest. He is far too intent on revenging himself on his betters."

She understood very well now why Ashton had snubbed her. The moment he received her grandfather's congratulations, he had known she had plotted against him.

For a moment, she permitted herself to believe it would be possible to go to him, to tell him that she really did love him, that she had plotted only because she wished to remain his wife, and for the best of reasons. But she knew she might as well bay at the moon. He would never believe anything she said now.

"You are very quiet, Bella," said her grandfather, who waited impatiently for her to echo his vilification of Ashton.

"Grandpapa, I am obliged to tell you what must grieve you: I never told Tassie that Ashton had changed his mind. How could I, when I have never heard anything to that effect?"

Even in the dim light, she could see the red spots flame her grandfather's sagging cheeks. He was a Wortwell, and Wortwells did not like to be crossed.

"Good God! That niece of mine has made a fool of me," he cried. "Not only did I congratulate Ashton on thinking better of the divorce, but I actually—" and here he choked "—*welcomed* him to the family!"

The irony of the situation did not escape Isabella, but she could not bring herself to smile. However, she did not propose to let the Old Duke see her tears, for he was no more renowned for his sympathy than the Prince was for his restraint.

His eyes bulged with fury. "I shall make that pea-brained cousin of yours rue the day she was so bold as to send me glad tidings!"

"You will please do no such thing," Isabella said. She was able to speak with every appearance of calm, for her own fate, she saw, was beyond saving. The wreckage that was her marriage must be put aside and not thought of until she might be private. For now, she must think of Tassie, who would not bear up well under the Old Duke's abuse and would make herself quite ill with self-pity for weeks afterward. "You will kindly keep mum," Isabella said. "I shall speak with Tassie myself."

The Old Duke would have flown into a temper at this, but Isabella forestalled him by saying soothingly, "Dear Grandpapa, I will not have you popping off in an apoplexy, which you are certain to do at your age if you shout at anybody."

He glared at her fiercely. "You have sworn to forget my age! If you allude to it again, I shall never speak to you."

"I shall engage to forget it entirely if you will leave Tassie to me. Meanwhile, you may play dice with Wild Goose."

"Ah, the Princess!" he cried. "An excellent suggestion! She will prove most useful. I shall use her to teach that fellow Ashton the lesson he sorely needs. He will learn that I can be as vengeful as he.''

Warily, Isabella asked, ''What do you intend to do?''

He gloated, ''I shall present Princess Wild Goose to the Regent. Her Royal Highness will receive every attention, as much as King Louis himself, while Ashton is entirely snubbed. It will be a delicious comeuppance.''

''You cannot present Wild Goose to the Prince,'' Isabella said with a sigh.

''Of course, I can. I have been very thick with Prinny of late. He will grant any request of mine, and, I daresay he will be quite delighted with the Princess, for her nobleness of mind is not often met with in this lax age.''

''True enough, but she is not a princess.''

He nearly rose out of his seat. ''Then why, pray, does she pass herself off as one?'' he bellowed.

''I am the one who passes her off as a princess. You would have been horrid to her if you had known she did not have any blood, and so I gave her the title.''

He harrumphed, pouted and banged his stick on the floor of the carriage. ''I shall have to sever the acquaintance at once. There is nothing for it but to give her up.''

''But Grandpapa, you like her so well. Surely, you would not give her up because she is not a princess.''

''Indeed I would,'' he contradicted. ''The only question that remains is whether I shall give *you* up as well!''

ON THE NEXT DAY, at the earliest opportunity, Isabella confessed to Tassie that her plan to win Ashton's heart had failed utterly.

"But I saw you and Tony together. He held you in his arms!" she cried. "I saw it with my own eyes."

"Half of London might see me in his arms," Isabella remarked. "It would signify nothing."

Tassie groaned. Then, as a new idea gripped her, she grew rigid with terror. "Oh, Bella, I told your grandfather that Ashton had changed his mind, that there would be no divorce. Do you suppose he believed me?"

Gently, Isabella replied, "I am afraid he did."

"Gracious me," said the good woman. "It occurs to me that somebody minded what I said!" She smiled with pleasure.

Isabella laughed. "Yes, and no less a personage than His Grace, the Duke of Wortwell. But Tassie—" and here her voice grew serious "—this must serve as a warning to you, for if there are those who are inclined to mind what you say, you had better, from this day forward, stick reasonably close to the truth."

Much struck with this heavy responsibility, Tassie wondered whether it was such a great thing after all to have one's opinion regarded higher than the snap of a finger.

ASHTON FOUND HIMSELF unaccountably restless—so much so that the following morning, before it was light, having failed to close his eyes the entire night, he dressed, left his rooms and walked the streets of the Town. No fewer than three minions of the law stopped him to deliver warnings that footpads, pickpockets and murderers were abroad and that the gentleman must have a care for his purse and his person. No fewer than four ladies of the evening solicited his custom, no fewer than five beggars implored his worship's charity, and one thief accosted him, only to be

sent fleeing for his life, thanks to a wrestling trick
Ashton had learned from Indian braves at Fort
George. But not one of these would-be assaults affected him as much as the knowledge that Isabella had
schemed against him.

As if to tempt the Fates, he entered Hyde Park,
strolling in the direction of the Serpentine, regardless
of any danger which might lurk in the shrubs. The real
danger was Bella's perfidy, he felt, and he had only
just barely escaped. He had actually believed that she
loved him, when, in fact, her sole aim had been to
avert the divorce. He owed much to the one man he
had never thought to thank—the Old Duke—who had
inadvertently saved him at the eleventh hour.

He could not deceive himself; he loved Isabella. He
wished he could regard that fact in the same way he
regarded a very bad cold, as a temporary condition,
one he had recovered from in the past and would do
so again. But he could not. When he had set sail for
the New World, he had been numb with grief. Now,
every nerve and fibre in him acknowledged that he
wanted Isabella.

The only antidote lay in the fields and farms at
Candover. He would go there that very day and think
what, if anything, could be done in the matter of the
divorce. He would throw himself into the manage-
ment of his estate. There were hops to be planted and
a charity school to be built. A host of undertakings
came to mind, relieving him from thoughts of Bella,
until he recollected that he could not immerse himself
in crops, tenancies or schools for a while yet. Nor
could he take himself where he would be sure of not
setting eyes upon his wife. He could not, because Celeste had engaged to play cricket.

THE DAY OF THE MATCH dawned grey and foggy, giving some the hope and others the fear that the event would be postponed. Such a calamity was no more than the planners and participants might have expected, for since the moment of its conception, the match had been twice cancelled, twice rescheduled and once moved to a new location. It was now to take place in Lord's New Cricket Ground, its sponsor to be the Marylebone Cricket Club. The eleven team members for each side included an array of feminine beauty from fourteen to forty, and the stakes had risen from fifty to five hundred guineas a side.

All these developments served to intensify Celeste's anxiety. A hundred times she threatened to withdraw. Only the gentle persuasions of Isabella succeeded in keeping her to her word. But when the poor girl saw the sun burst out from behind the clouds on the day of the match, an expression of such gloom spread across her pretty face that Isabella could not help but pity her and Wild Goose could not help but offer her a bit of turnip.

"All will be well. You shall see," Isabella assured the girl, as Chad drove them all to the cricket ground.

Unfortunately, Isabella could not encourage Celeste with any conviction. She sensed that the girl might make herself sick with fear and, if such a catastrophe were to transpire, Isabella would have only herself to blame. She had been remiss in keeping her promise to teach Celeste to play cricket. Wishing to avoid Ashton, she had sought a way out of her promise, and to that end, she had hit on the happy expedient of asking Chad to take her place as teacher. Fortunately for her, the dear boy had overcome his natural diffidence and agreed.

The team members met in the tent near the playing ground for the purpose of reviewing their attire and strategy. Wild Goose assisted Celeste in hitching up her skirts so that she might not trip over them. Inspecting the results, Isabella saw that even if Celeste were the worst player ever to bowl or to bat, the shapeliness of her ankles would win her the applause of the spectators.

Next, Isabella and Wild Goose adjusted the girl's bootlaces and, as the day was growing warm, rolled up her white sleeves. Finally, they tied back Celeste's curls beneath a fetching cap. Stepping back to appraise her, Isabella pronounced her ready. Celeste closed her eyes and announced that she was about to be sick.

Wild Goose intoned a chant over her head while Isabella scolded, "You shall not be ill. Think how disappointed Chad will be if, after all the hours he has spent teaching you, it comes to nothing."

Red-faced and ashamed, Celeste thought better of being sick. Summoning her courage, she permitted Isabella to take her by the hand and lead her from the tent. Outside, Isabella was required to steady the girl with both hands, for upon seeing the number of spectators and hearing their cheers and applause, she nearly turned and fled into the tent once more.

"Do not look at them," Isabella advised.

Celeste could not tear her eyes from the brightly dressed crowd with its yapping dogs, prancing horses, open carriages, picnic baskets, champagne glasses, colourful banners and cheerful grins.

"Look at the bowler's wicket," Isabella said, pointing the girl's head in the direction of the playing ground. Her team-mates stood nearby, waiting for her to approach.

Obediently, Celeste squinted and fixed her eyes on the two-stump wicket.

Isabella steered her towards her team-mates. "Remember, all will be well, as long as you look at the wicket," she said.

Because she carried out this instruction to the letter, Celeste did not see Guy and Lady Suppel, who waved to her from the boundary fence. Isabella was forced to wave to them in her stead. Celeste also did not see Chad, who had been joined by Wild Goose and now smiled encouragement at her. Therefore, Isabella had to deliver him an answering smile by proxy. Nor did Celeste see Ashton, who, from atop his horse, threw a posy in her direction. Isabella saw it, however, and retrieved the posy. When her eyes met his, his jaw tightened. After a heavy pause, he spurred his horse and rode off.

At last the game began. Isabella moved Celeste to her playing position near the popping crease. Then, leaving the field, Isabella went to join Guy and Lady Suppel.

During the first innings, it was clear that the bowling was such that batting would dominate the play. The bowlers were pretty, lusty females, who played with energy, but if they ever managed to throw the ball far enough, they could not get it to break or swerve so as to prevent the batter from hitting it. Consequently, a great many runs were scored.

As batsman, Celeste scarcely dared look at the ball. Nevertheless, to her astonishment, she contrived on her first attempt to knock the balls off the wicket and score a run. From that moment, she was transformed into so eager a player that she was guilty of leg before wicket, a piece of interference she repeated several times over. Happily, the umpire found her too charming to do more than give her a pretty scold.

The prodigious number of runs set the crowd to cheering. One of the dogs who entertained himself by chasing balls along the boundary fence was inspired by the noise to leap onto the playing ground. He caught a tossed ball in his teeth and off he ran with it across the lawn, finally disappearing behind the tent.

Ashton, who was observing the match from atop his horse, laughed at the rascal pup and vowed to the clubsmen that he would retrieve their stolen ball. On that, he rode after the hound and was soon lost to view. Thus, he was far off when Celeste miscalculated the opposing batter's move, so that when she ran to catch the ball, she caught it in the side of her head.

Instantly, she crumpled to the grass. Almost as instantly, Chad was there. He gathered the girl in his arms and, before the stunned crowd could find its voice, he disappeared with her into the tent. Wild Goose swiftly followed.

For a moment, everyone froze. When they came to life again, they considered whether the surgeon ought to be summoned. Before they could decide, the gentlemen who had bet on the match bethought themselves that they could not very well win any blunt unless the game went forward. They, therefore, found a buxom young girl of fifteen to take Celeste's place, escorted her out to the wicket-keeper to receive her instructions and called for the game to proceed.

Because Guy had wandered off with Lady Suppel and a bottle of champagne, he was unaware of what had occurred, but Isabella had witnessed the entire scene. As quickly as she could, she hurried to the tent, all the time blaming herself for not tending better to Celeste. She ought to have been the one to teach the girl. Chad was good-hearted and generous, but he did not know the dangers of the game as she did. Experienced as she was in playing, she could have warned the girl of possible pitfalls and missteps. She could have drilled her in methods of safety. She could have prevented the tragedy.

Opening the flap of the tent, Isabella stood stock-still. Celeste lay on a bench. Chad knelt beside her. He cradled her head in his arms, kissed her forehead repeatedly and cried, "Oh, my darling, my darling!"

Meanwhile, Celeste wept tears from large, adoring eyes, kissed the air when she could not reach his cheek and replied, "Oh, my dearest, my dearest!"

Putting her hand to her forehead, Isabella moaned, "Oh, my God, my God!"

BECAUSE THEY WERE too engrossed in each other to hear that last exclamation, they continued to exchange kisses and endearments until Isabella summoned their attention. "My dear Miss DuChateau," she stated loudly, causing the two of them to jump out of their skins, "your wound has obviously rendered you too delirious to know what you are saying. And you," she said darkly to Chad, "your behaviour is inexcusable."

Shamefaced, he stood and helped Celeste to rise, as well. She bore a red mark on the side of her face which promised to blossom into a purple bruise.

"I love her," Chad said simply.

Isabella's fury would have burst forth then, showing her for the Wortwell she was, but Celeste ran forward and grasped her hands, pleading, "Do not be angry with him. I am the one at fault. I love him with all my heart. I loved him the first moment I saw him, and I made so bold as to tell him so. Do not blame him.''

No longer shamefaced, Chad stood his full height, which was considerably more than Isabella had estimated, and he approached the two ladies. Firmly, he put a protective arm about Celeste's shoulder and said, ''It does not matter that she was the first to speak. I loved her before she said a word. If she had not spoken, I would have.''

For the first time, Isabella's eyes fell on Wild Goose, who stood behind the lovers with her arms folded, beaming at the entire proceeding.

''Why didn't you stop them?'' Isabella cried.

Wild Goose, still beaming, replied, ''I am *yatoro*. I see that young girl fulfils desire of the soul.''

Isabella stamped her foot. ''You are a chaperone. You are supposed to see that a young girl does *not* fulfil desire of the soul.''

''Boy and girl must marry,'' Wild Goose pronounced, with a shaking of the head. ''They wish to marry. Is the way of nature.''

Desperately, Isabella implored Celeste, ''How can you agree to marry without consulting your cousin or your brother? Did it never occur to you that they might have had a higher destiny in mind for you? Do you think only of yourself? And as for you,'' she shot at Chad, ''how can you, of all people, betray my trust in you?''

Though the two young people scarcely understood this reproach, they begged forgiveness.

''What is so dreadful,'' Isabella cried, clenching her fists, ''is that Ashton will suffer.''

Celeste gazed at Chad in puzzlement. ''How can our happiness harm him?'' she asked.

"He is in love with you," Isabella cried. Then, turning to Chad, she said, "Do you understand? Ashton is in love with her."

"Oh!" Celeste cried in anguish. "I am so sorry. But after all, he is married—to you, Mrs. Ashton."

"I know very well he is married to me, but I have promised to assist him in obtaining a divorce. I will not allow his heart to be broken, not again, and so you must give each other up."

"No!" the other three answered with one voice.

For the next ten minutes, she expostulated with them, invoked every mistake she had ever made in the past which showed the folly of acting out of wilfulness, selfishness and a youthful insistence upon having what one wants the instant one wants it. She implored them, each in turn, to consider those who would be hurt by their rash action, namely Ashton, who had always acted with the utmost benevolence towards them all. "He might have cut you, Chad, on account of your father's reputation," she said urgently, "but he was above such unworthy sentiments. And you, Celeste, has he not always put your wishes first? Is this how you repay him?"

Throughout the lecture, the lovers listened, nodded sorrowfully and agreed that no two people existed on the planet who were more treacherous, wicked and ungrateful than themselves. But when Isabella asked them to think better of announcing an engagement or marrying anytime soon, they clapped their mouths shut and would not budge. They would grant that every epithet Isabella or the world might bestow on them was true; nevertheless, they would not consent to part. To add to Isabella's despair, Wild Goose was adamant that it was the first duty of young people to fulfil the desire of their souls.

Isabella tried to think what to do. At last, she collected herself and said, "Promise me you will do nothing and say nothing to anybody about this until we have spoken again. Promise that you will come to me tomorrow so that we may decide what is best to do."

"We will promise," Chad said boldly, "if you will make us a promise in return."

Amazed at this brazenness, Isabella had to repress the desire to shake him. "What is it you wish?" she asked.

"Please speak to Ashton for us," he said. "Explain to him all that has happened and that we never meant to harm anybody. Induce him, if you can, to receive us."

Stunned, Isabella was silent, giving Celeste the opportunity to say, "Oh, please do explain to him. No one can accomplish it as well as you can. He will listen to you, and you may comfort him. I would never wish him to seek a divorce on my account. Nor do I wish him to be angry with us. Oh, please say you will speak with him." On that plea, the girl dissolved into tears.

It gave Isabella a pang to know that they regarded her as she had earlier regarded herself: as having the power to influence Ashton.

Before she could explain that she was the last creature he would give an ear to, Ashton himself stepped into the tent. His face was alive with concern as he went to Celeste and took her hand. "I heard there had been an accident. I have sent for the surgeon." He stopped speaking, looked at the faces which stared at him and sensed the electricity filling the tent. "What is the matter?" he asked.

CHAPTER NINETEEN

"I FEAR I MAY be sick," Celeste rasped.

"She was hit by the ball," Chad explained.

"We make preparations for wedding feast," Wild Goose answered.

"Nothing is the matter!" Isabella insisted.

Because they all spoke at once and their words were a jumble, Ashton regarded them with some amusement. "Come," he said tenderly to Celeste. Taking her hand and putting it on his arm, he led her and Wild Goose out of the tent. As he left, he turned and said to Chad, "Thank you for looking after her in my absence." He glanced at Isabella. Though it cost him an effort, he said, "Thank you for assisting my cousin." The next instant they were gone.

Alone, Isabella and Chad exchanged a glance. Neither spoke. Holding open the flap of the tent, he waited for Isabella to pass through. He then followed. Without a word, they manoeuvred their way among the crowd, which was too wild with cheering the match to notice them. Silently, they rode in the carriage to Hertford Street. In the hall, they parted, Chad to his chamber, Isabella to her sitting-room. As neither appeared at the dinner table that evening, Tassie ate alone, accompanied only by the thought that if she lived in Cornwall with no society but the sheep's, life could not be more dull.

THE NEXT DAY, Isabella awaited the arrival of the two young people with greater calm than she had been able to summon the previous afternoon. Indeed, she even began to feel hopeful. They were not bad children, after all; they were merely young and headstrong. If she was patient and kind, if she kept her temper and let them know how completely she understood their passion for each other, she was certain to bring them round to a rational way of thinking. Their good hearts and excellent characters would be eloquent on the side of right. In the end, they would be persuaded to wait, to think before speaking to Ashton or anyone else and to behave like sensible creatures.

Full of anticipation, Isabella ordered that tea be brought to the drawing-room as soon as the young people should arrive. Chad's favourite cakes were to adorn the tray. Celeste's favourite sandwiches were to form a fragrant pyramid on a gilt-edged plate. With everything in readiness, Isabella had only to wait.

Time passed and no one appeared save Tassie, who watched as Isabella stood and paced, sat and drummed her fingers, peered out of the window, all in an effort to hurry their arrival. An hour passed, then two, and they did not appear. Weary with fretting, she dozed off in a chair by the fire, and when she awoke, it was too late for tea.

The servant who came in to light the lamps was sent to Chad's room with a note. Moments later, he returned bearing the news that Mr. Mattingly must have gone out.

Isabella left the drawing-room at a run to go to the young man's bedchamber. As there was no answer to her knock, she tried the door. It gave way and she went inside. The open drawers, cabinets and wardrobe told her at once that he had not merely gone out; he had gone and taken his belongings with him.

She sat on the bed for a moment, took a deep breath and decided what needed to be done. Then, rising, she went to do it.

AT UPPER BERKELEY STREET, she was informed that neither Miss DuChateau nor her brother was at home. The latter had gone out with Lady Suppel. The former had gone to the country and was not expected for several days.

"Why did you not stop her?" Isabella cried to the butler.

Raising his brows, he explained that it was not his place to say anything regarding the comings and goings of his betters, though if he were permitted to venture an opinion, he would have a great deal to say on the subject, and none of it very good.

Regretting that she had spoken impulsively, Isabella thanked him for his information, placed a coin in his palm and would have returned to her carriage, but the servant asked if she wished to be announced to Wild Goose, who was within.

She was ushered into a large saloon where Wild Goose sat at supper with the Old Duke. At the sight of his granddaughter, he rose and hastened forward to greet her, explaining in a whisper, "I did mean to give her up, but I cannot. She amuses me far too much, and what is more, she is a tonic. My gout has never been better."

Isabella smiled.

"You will not say anything about her not being a princess, will you?" he said in a low voice. "The world regards her as a princess; we might as well keep mum."

"Yes. As I am the one who elevated her, it is in my interest to keep the secret."

Relieved, the duke resumed his seat at the table and attacked his beefsteak and pudding with more appetite than Isabella had seen him evince in many a year.

Approaching Wild Goose, she asked, "Is it true? Has Celeste gone to the country?"

Gravely, Wild Goose acknowledged it was true.

"And did Mr. Mattingly accompany her?"

"He did."

"I must go and see Mr. Ashton at once."

"Ah, you also fulfil desire of the soul?"

Isabella shook her head, then took her leave.

"Well, I for one am always happy to take your advice, Princess," declared the Old Duke. On that, he fulfilled the desire of *his* soul and took a long swallow from his glass of wine.

ISABELLA DIRECTED the coachman to drive to Ashton's lodgings. Then, sitting back, she steeled herself for an encounter she had wished desperately to avoid. She need not have distressed herself, however, for upon reaching her destination, she learned that the master had left for Candover immediately following the cricket match, and there was no telling when he intended to return.

THE SOUTHWEST WING of Candover consisted of the remains of an early Tudor house, half-timbered with an overhanging upper storey and three gables. In 1575, the owner had added onto the house, completing the northwest facade in brick with stone dressings. In the eighteenth century, the house was bought by a banker, who employed Repton to add bays to the south front and a garden with gurgling stream and topiary trees to the east. Thomas Jones was brought in by the next owner to add a sleek modern section to the north with porch and two-transomed windows. This delightful hodgepodge had been purchased by Simon Ashton so that he might have an estate to pass on to his heir. That heir now sat in the sunny south parlour, studying an account book to the accompaniment of a hound snoring at his feet, a canary singing in the bright window, and the housekeeper humming "Robin Adair" as she arranged flowers in a bowl.

Into this harmonious scene came a footman to announce Mrs. Ashton, who did not wait for the servant to finish speaking her name but dashed in out of breath and said in a tense voice, "Tony."

His expression was severe, and he did not greet her by word. He stood and took a step towards her. Looking round at the housekeeper, he indicated with his eyes that she might be excused.

When Mrs. Ducking saw the master and the mistress standing together in the same room at the same moment for the first time in far too many years, she dipped a curtsy, clasped her hands to her bosom and bustled joyfully from the room.

The hound, who had awakened when Ashton moved his feet, also recognized that the master and mistress were now in unaccustomed proximity, and he sat on his haunches, put out his tongue expectantly and watched.

The canary, oblivious to everything, warbled a hymn to the sunshine.

"Something has happened," Isabella said.

Seeing her agitation, he responded, "You had better sit." He led her to the sofa by a tall window and sat by her side.

He looked at her so steadily that she was obliged to glance down at her hands, which she tried in vain to keep from wringing. "You must prepare yourself, Tony. I have very bad news."

Calmly, he waited for her to go on.

"I am so sorry. I tried to prevent it, but I could not. Chad and Celeste. They have fallen in love."

An expression of puzzlement crossed his handsome face. "You tried to prevent it?"

She coloured. His question told her that he did not believe her. It mortified her to know that he had good reason to think her a liar. "I spoke with both of them, I assure you. I put before them all the rational arguments against their forming an attachment, especially when they are so young and so likely to repent of any rash decision in years to come."

"Well, and what did they say to that?"

Isabella eye's filled as she contemplated the abysmal failure of her arguments. "They refused to part."

"Well, I suppose that settles it, then."

This struck Isabella as a shockingly lukewarm response. "Is that all you have to say?"

"What more is there to say? They have evidently made up their minds."

"But you love her. You told me you wished to marry her!"

"Obviously, that is out of the question now."

Taking a breath, she shook her head sorrowfully. "Do not do this, Tony." Her voice was low and full of emotion. "Do not let Celeste go. I beg you."

His face showed his surprise.

Before he could speak, she went on. "You cannot simply throw up your hands, acquiesce and go off to the New World or wherever it is you mean to go this time. You cannot permit her to think that her fate is of no concern to you. You must find her and do everything in your power to make her stay."

"And exactly how am I to do that?"

"Tell her that you love her."

"Is that all? It scarcely seems enough when she is so determined to have another."

Her intensity left her breathless. "Tell her that you love her and do not want her to go."

After a pause, he replied, "You need not distress yourself, Bella. I shall not make that mistake twice."

She lowered her eyes, thankful that he had not resented her interference. "There is one more thing. I'm afraid you will have to go after her. I believe they have gone to Gretna Green."

"I am quite certain they haven't."

"I know Chad appears too quiet and studious a young man ever to induce a young girl to elope, but he is very much in love. He wishes to marry her."

"I know."

Amazed, she stood. "You know?"

He rose as well. "Yes. No doubt they thought they could not possibly find a more unsympathetic listener in me than they had found in you, and so they told me everything."

After absorbing this news, Isabella pressed her lips together. "I see," she said grimly. "Then I am superfluous." She turned to leave him, but when she reached the door, she found Ashton already there, blocking her way.

"There was one point of information they omitted," he said.

His ironic look made her think better of asking what it was.

"They neglected to tell me that you tried to prevent their marrying, and of all the facts in the case, I find that the most interesting."

She backed away, feeling cornered.

"Why did you try to prevent it?" he asked.

"I wished to spare you a broken heart, I suppose."

"Why?" As she moved back, he moved towards her.

Her eyes scanned the room, as though the answer to his question were emblazoned on the walls. "I don't know," she said. "I suppose because you have already had it broken once. It is someone else's turn now."

"Whose turn?" By this time, he had backed her against a table and there was nowhere left to retreat to.

"I don't know."

He was so close that she felt his breath on her hair. "Whose turn, Bella?"

Swallowing, she said, "Well, perhaps Chad's heart ought to be broken. It would season him, give him strength of character."

"Come now, Bella. You are a better liar than that. Whose heart ought to be broken?"

"Well, there's Tassie. One might easily break her heart by transporting her to Cornwall."

"The truth. Whose heart?"

Helplessly, she closed her eyes. "King George's," she said.

The next instant, his hands caressed her face and his lips pressed hard on hers. When he let her go, he held her away and said, "For once, tell me truth, straight out, without disguise."

"Oh, Tony, I should like nothing better, but I am sorely out of practice."

"Then I'll begin. Bella, I love you and I do not want you to go."

Stunned, she waited, as though expecting him to retract the words.

"Now it is your turn. You love me. Say it."

She bowed her head. "Yes."

"That is why you wished to prevent the divorce."

"Yes."

"Not because you wished to please your grandfather."

"When have you known me ever to please my grandfather?"

"And not because you feared Mr. Doty would discover you had lied about Philip Mattingly?"

"No."

"The full truth, Bella."

Mustering her courage, she said, "I love you. I love you so much, Tony, that I can scarcely say the words, for they scarcely express what I feel."

He kissed her hand. "I thought you loved me, but I was not entirely certain until I heard all your excellent advice regarding my courtship of Celeste."

"I hope with all my heart that you will not be courting anybody."

"Excepting yourself, of course."

"I make a vow, Tony. There shall be no more stratagems, no more plots, no more lies. Henceforth, I shall tell you everything directly and without disguise."

"And henceforth, I shall keep my feet planted next to yours, so that I may hear every pearl of truth which falls from your lips."

Each extended a hand towards the other so that they might shake hands on the bargain.

"Tony," she said, "there is something else I must tell you."

"Good God, more truth! I do believe we have opened Pandora's box."

"What I am about to say is more than truthful. It is historic. Indeed, I am surely the first Wortwell ever to utter such blasphemy."

"I had better sit, lest I be overcome!" After doing so, he drew her down close beside him. "I am quite prepared now," he said. "You may proceed."

"What I have to confess is this: I am sorry, deeply sorry."

He nodded. "We both have much to regret."

"I ought to have known you missed him as dreadfully as I did. I ought to have had a thought for your sorrow."

"There is much I ought to have done, as well. And because I did not do it then, I think it fitting that I begin to do it now." He stretched his arm around her shoulder, and with a gentle hand, induced her to rest her head against his breast. When she looked up at him, he lightly kissed her eyes, whereupon she reached up to kiss his lips. When they had done kissing, he inhaled the perfume of her hair; she nestled close.

They continued in this vein for a considerable length of time, so that when they retired, hand in hand, the housekeeper, who had overheard the entire proceeding, was able to report below stairs, with tears of thanksgiving, that all was well, for the master and mistress were, at long last, perfectly cosy.

Following the success of WITH THIS RING, Harlequin cordially invites you to enjoy the romance of the wedding season with

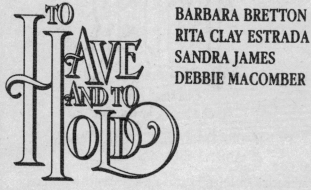

TO HAVE AND TO HOLD

BARBARA BRETTON
RITA CLAY ESTRADA
SANDRA JAMES
DEBBIE MACOMBER

A collection of romantic stories that celebrate the joy, excitement, and mishaps of planning that special day by these four award-winning Harlequin authors.

Available in April at your favorite Harlequin retail outlets.

HARLEQUIN PROUDLY PRESENTS A
DAZZLING CONCEPT IN ROMANCE FICTION

One small town,
twelve terrific love stories.

TYLER—GREAT READING... GREAT SAVINGS...
AND A FABULOUS FREE GIFT

Each book set in Tyler is a self-contained love story;
together, the twelve novels stitch the fabric of
the community.

By collecting proofs-of-purchase found in each Tyler
book, you can receive a fabulous gift, ABSOLUTELY
FREE! And use our special Tyler coupons to save on
your next Tyler book purchase.

Join us for the third Tyler book, WISCONSIN
WEDDING by Carla Neggers, available in May.

TAKE A LESSON FROM RUTH LANGAN, BRONWYN WILLIAMS, LYNDA TRENT AND MARIANNE WILLMAN . . .

A *history* lesson! These and many more of your favorite authors are waiting to sweep you into the world of conquistadors and countesses, pioneers and pirates. In Harlequin Historicals, you'll rediscover the romance of the past, from the Great Crusades to the days of the Gibson girls, with four exciting, sensuous stories each month.

So pick up a Harlequin Historical and travel back in time with some of the best writers in romance.... Don't let history pass you by!

® **Harlequin** ®

JANELLE TAYLOR

Valley of Fire

HARLEQUIN IS PROUD TO PRESENT *VALLEY OF FIRE* BY JANELLE TAYLOR—AUTHOR OF TWENTY-TWO BOOKS, INCLUDING SIX *NEW YORK TIMES* BESTSELLERS

VALLEY OF FIRE—the warm and passionate story of Kathy Alexander, a famous romance author, and Steven Winngate, entrepreneur and owner of the magazine that intended to expose the real Kathy "Brandy" Alexander to her fans.

Don't miss VALLEY OF FIRE, available in May.

FREE GIFT OFFER

To receive your free gift, send us the specified number of proofs-of-purchase from any specially marked Free Gift Offer Harlequin or Silhouette book with the Free Gift Certificate properly completed. plus a check or money order (do not send cash) to cover postage and handling payable to Harlequin/Silhouette Free Gift Promotion Offer. We will send you the specified gift.

FREE GIFT CERTIFICATE

ITEM	A. GOLD TONE EARRINGS	B. GOLD TONE BRACELET	C. GOLD TONE NECKLACE
# of proofs-of-purchase required	3	6	9
Postage and Handling	$1.75	$2.25	$2.75
Check one	☐	☐	☐

Name: _____

Address: _____

City: _____ State: _____ Zip Code: _____

Mail this certificate. specified number of proofs-of-purchase and a check or money order for postage and handling to: HARLEQUIN/SILHOUETTE FREE GIFT OFFER 1992, P.O. Box 9057, Buffalo, NY 14269-9057. Requests must be received by July 31, 1992.

PLUS—Every time you submit a completed certificate with the correct number of proofs-of-purchase, you are automatically entered in our MILLION DOLLAR SWEEPSTAKES! No purchase or obligation necessary to enter. See below for alternate means of entry and how to obtain complete sweepstakes rules.

✄ HG1U

ONE PROOF-OF-PURCHASE
To collect your fabulous FREE GIFT you must include the necessary FREE GIFT proofs-of-purchase with a properly completed offer certificate.

(See center insert for details)